Clarity 5

Loving Liam

by
Loretta Lost

ISBN-13: 978-1532901522
ISBN-10: 1532901526

Only a child sees things with perfect clarity because it hasn't developed all those filters which prevent us from seeing things that we don't expect to see.

Douglas Adams

Table of Contents

Prologue

Liam Larson, 1989

I am standing on the side of the road and holding a newborn infant.

She is looking up at me with curiosity on her face, and I can already tell she's going to be my best friend. We're going to do everything together, especially coloring and making snow angels. She's really tiny right now, but I'm sure that when she's a little bigger she'll love playing catch with me. I have a ball, but I don't have anyone to play with.

First, I need to know her name.

"What are we going to call her, Mama?"

Turning to the side, I look at my mother who is sitting in the driver's seat of the car and crying softly. I think she's crying because it hurt a lot to take the baby out of her stomach. There is blood staining her dress, and she is clutching her midsection as her shoulders shake with sobs. She barely makes any sound, but she is shaking so hard that the car is trembling beneath her.

Loretta Lost

I thought she needed to go to the hospital, but she said no.

The baby in my arms is bloody and red. Maybe that's why Mama never wanted to touch her. When she came out, I tried to wipe most of the gooey stuff off her before wrapping her up in Mama's green sweater. Once I got it all off her face, I was able to see that she's perfect. She has clear blue eyes and chubby little fingers. Her bellybutton was funny. I asked Mama what to do about the floppy string, but she wouldn't help me.

"Liam," my mother says from the car, and she is crying so much that she can hardly breathe. "Leave her there. Hurry! Before someone drives by."

I look around in confusion. It's early morning, and there aren't many other cars on the road. Why would Mama want me to leave the baby here? It's winter and there is a thin layer of snow on the ground. I shift the baby in my arms, because they are growing tired. She might be tiny, but I'm not that big and strong yet and it's hard to hold her.

"Please, Liam," my mother says again, placing her face in her hands as though she cannot look at me. "Put the baby down and come back into the car."

"I don't want to. She'll be cold."

My mother wipes her face on her sleeve, trying to remove some of the tears and clean her runny nose. She sits up a little straighter and grasps the steering wheel tightly. "Liam, if you don't get your ass back here this instant I'll tell your father that you disobeyed me. He'll give you a good beating!"

I flinch at this prospect, and hug the baby tighter against my chest. I don't want Papa to hit me anymore. He's been away for a little while, but I know he'll be back soon, and he'll start hurting me again.

"For god's sake, Liam," my mother whispers desperately. "If you don't do as I say, your father will kill me. He's going to strangle me to death, and who knows what he'll do to the baby. He *hates* little girls."

She's right. I have seen my father choke my mother before, and he always says mean things about girls. I begin to grow very afraid. Will he treat the baby in my arms even worse than he treats me? If putting her down means she won't get punched or kicked by Papa, is that better? Somehow, she feels glued to my chest, and I don't want to let her go; not for anything.

"Please," my mother says frantically as she waves me over with her hand. "Please just leave the baby there."

"But… but she'll get hurt. If cars drive by, they could hit her."

"We'll come back for her, soon. I promise. I just need to go home. I'm in a lot of pain."

I look down at the ground fearfully. "Are you sure, Mama?"

"*Leave her,* Liam!"

Loretta Lost

I quickly move to do as she says, and place the baby down in the snow on the side of the road. The little girl looks at me in confusion as I stand up, and her tiny arms move a little, reaching out for me. I can tell she already misses the warmth of being held; she misses me. My heart is breaking. This feels wrong.

"Quickly, Liam!" my mother shouts.

Ripping my own coat off my shoulders, I lay it over the baby as an extra layer of protection. She makes a cooing sound as she looks up at me, and I feel tears falling from my eyes onto her cheeks. "I love you," I tell her, bending down to place a kiss on her forehead. "I'm sorry. We'll come back for you, little sister. Mama promised." I have a terrible feeling, but I'm too afraid to go against my mother, so I run back to the car. I can hear the baby start to cry, and my chest aches.

I have barely jumped into the vehicle before my mom starts driving away. I didn't even get a chance to close my car door, but it slams shut with the force of the car's acceleration. My mother is sobbing and the car is veering dangerously as she drives away at breakneck speeds.

"Mama?" I ask her nervously. "Are we gonna go back for her soon?"

"Who?" my mother asks brokenly.

"The baby."

"What baby?" Tears pour down my mother's face as she shakes her head violently. "There is no baby. There never was a baby."

4

Her words confuse me, and I look behind the car to try to see where I laid the infant down on the side of the road. I can still hear her cries echoing in my ears. I can still see her sweet face looking up at me. "Mama, we have to go back," I say as panic begins to fill my chest. "I left the baby there and it's so cold. She doesn't even have clothes yet. Can we go back now?"

"There is no baby," my mother says quietly, repeating the words to herself over and over. "There is no baby."

I am terrified. There's something wrong with my mother and I don't know what to do. What's going to happen now? Is my little sister going to be okay? I am her big brother. I was supposed to protect her.

What have I done?

Chapter One

Helen Winters

Lifting the slender plastic stick between my thumb and forefinger, I brace myself for life-changing news. Before I can even read the results, I clamp my eyes shut tightly. I'm not ready for this. I haven't accomplished enough or traveled enough. I haven't lived enough, learned enough, or seen nearly enough—heck, I've only been able to see at all for a few short months!

I am not sure how it is possible to want something so badly and be so frightened at the same time. This is going to change everything. Am I responsible enough? I crashed my car into a tree not too long ago, like a complete fool. I still occasionally drink whole bottles of wine all by myself. Am I old enough? I still feel like this is all so sudden and I am too young, but I know that my body is already past its prime for childbearing. Reading articles about the decline of egg quality with maternal age has really scared me, along with my sister losing her baby at twenty-nine. I know that those were extenuating circumstances, but her pregnancy was difficult even before she was drugged. Am I already too old?

It doesn't matter. I need to try.

Opening one eye, I peek at the stick.

Dammit. All of the air I've been holding in my lungs leaves my chest in a gust. Am I sighing in disappointment or relief? I'm not sure. Tossing the stick into the trash can, I move to wash my hands in the sink and splash some cold water on my face. I towel off before moving toward the bedroom with heavy feet. Liam is sprawled on the bed, half-naked and half-asleep, and I pause to gaze at his body for a moment. He is so wonderful. It should be normal by now, but every single day, I find myself feeling a renewed thankfulness for my eyesight. And, of course, for Liam.

He has given me so much. I feel so awful and guilty that I don't have any good news to tell him. As I study his features in the dim morning light, I can't help fantasizing about what our children would look like. They would be so beautiful, brilliant, and strong.

Is there something wrong with me? We've been trying for months. My period is ten days late, and I thought for sure that things would be different this time. Is it possible that the test is wrong? I used my first morning urine, and it's supposed to be over 99% accurate. Moving over to sit on the bed beside Liam, I reach out and run my hand over his back.

He looks up at me at once, blinking the sleep out of his eyes.

"Hey, Helly-Belly," he says with a drowsy smile.

"Liam!" I glower at him. "You are never to call me that, on pain of death. I thought I made that clear the last time."

"Aw, come here," he says, reaching up to drag me down onto the bed for a hug. "You like me way too much to kill me."

Sulking, I let him wrap his arms around me and plant kisses along my shoulder before I share the results of my test. "It's still negative," I say quietly.

He pauses and lifts his head. "It can take a while, Helen. We just have to keep trying. Maybe it's for the best that it's hasn't happened."

"For the best? I thought you wanted to have a baby."

"I did. I do," Liam reaches up and runs a hand through his thick dark hair. "I mean, our wedding is in two weeks. Maybe we should just focus on getting everything ready for the ceremony and enjoying our honeymoon first. You won't be able to enjoy the vineyards of France if you are throwing up all the time, and you won't be able to taste any of the wines."

Pulling away a little, I turn over to look at him curiously. "Liam, is there something wrong? You were so excited about starting a family before that you didn't want to wait. Now you seem hesitant.

Are you having second thoughts?"

Liam looks down and away from me, and I can't read his expression. "I guess something has been bothering me lately," he admits softly. "You know me so well. I just didn't know how to talk to you about it."

My heart skips a beat. After everything that has happened lately, it's easy to feel fear. Our lives have been near paradise and perfection, and it's hard to believe they could continue like this unchecked. What disaster is waiting to strike me down this time? I try to push my doubts aside as I reach out to place a hand on Liam's chest. "What's bothering you?" I ask him gently, trying to be supportive. Is he cheating on me? Is he backing out of our wedding? Is it something to do with his parents? Is there something wrong with his health? Oh god, I bet he has cancer.

"It's just…" he begins, but trails off into silence. He shakes his head and moves away from me, throwing his legs off the bed and rising to his feet. "Never mind. It's stupid."

"Liam," I say, swallowing down the lump in my throat. "Tell me." I can't deal with secrets anymore. I can't deal with drama. We are about to be married, and I thought we were past all of this. We are trying to be *parents*, for god's sake. We need to have some kind of emotional stability.

"Give me a minute to wake up," Liam says, rubbing his eyes. "I am going to go put on some coffee." With that, he walks out of the room, leaving me a mess of nerves.

Lying back on the bed, I stare at the ceiling. Since Carmen found out that she might never be able to have children, I have felt as though the future of our family rests on my shoulders. She was ready to be a mother, and my father was excited to meet his first grandchild before everything fell apart. Even if I'm not totally ready, I know that my child will grow up with loving relatives. My family has been through so much heartache lately, and they are desperately in need of some love and laughter. A child could bring some joy and excitement back into our lives, and be the glue that holds us all together.

In the past, when life became challenging, I was quick to run away and abandon everyone. I can't change the past, and erase how weak I was. I can't take back the way that I hurt and disappointed those who loved me. I know that I neglected my father and let his health decline, even while he was funding research to help cure my blindness. I know that if I hadn't left, Carmen wouldn't have married Grayson. I have felt guilty for so long, knowing that I was a terrible daughter and sister. I am lucky that they still welcomed me back into their lives with open arms.

Now, I have Liam, and I feel stronger than ever. I was excited to take this step with him, finally moving forward into adulthood and trying to make up for everything I've done. But why does it feel like something is in the way? Why is there always something in the way?

Liam returns to the room, and begins to open drawers. I sit up in bed and watch him rushing around, feeling confused.

"I'm sorry," he says with a glance up at me as he pulls on his pants. "I have to go into work earlier than expected this morning. I don't even have time to shower. Can we talk about this later?"

"No. Tell me now."

"Helen…"

"Liam. Seriously. You have been trying to get me pregnant for three months and now you tell me that it's for the best that it hasn't happened? What are you hiding from me? Have you been crushing up birth control and putting it in my food? Did you get a vasectomy and fail to tell me?"

"Helen, that's all ridiculous," he says as he slides his arms into his jacket. He seems like he is trying to smile, but his lips are too tired and heavy to move. "It's nothing sinister like that, but I really need to get going."

"Do not walk out that door without explaining yourself," I warn him. "There will be consequences."

He hesitates. "Okay. If you must know… it's kind of strange. I've been having these awful dreams lately, about holding a baby. It's a recurring nightmare I used to have when I was younger, but it went away after a while. I guess I'd still get the dream once every couple years, but since we started trying to conceive and talking about parenthood…

it's been every damn night."

"A nightmare?" I ask him in puzzlement.

"Yes. It's really fucked up. In the dream, my mother keeps telling me…" Liam shakes his head, as though it's too painful to talk about. "It's weird, Helen. Sometimes it's so realistic that I swear it actually happened, but that's impossible. My mom was driving a car in the dream, and she doesn't know how to drive. She's too afraid to get anywhere near the driver's seat."

I squint my eyes a little as I look at Liam. It is clear that he is extremely disturbed by this nightmare, and I don't know how to comfort him. We've been so happy lately, and I haven't seen that tormented look on his face since the day we visited his father. I want to ask about the details of the dream, but I don't want to upset him. "Have you tried talking to your mother about it?"

Liam nods and looks down. "Have you met my mother? She just ignores me and stares into space. I was hoping that after I removed her cataracts and her vision improved, she would start to talk more, but she's still so scared. After I asked her about my dream, she spoke to me even less." He hesitates. "But the dreams have come more frequently since I started spending more time with her."

"Do you think it's due to some unresolved issues with your family?" I ask him.

"Yeah," he says, with a roll of his eyes. "My unresolved issue is that my father is still alive, and not in jail where he can no longer harm my mother."

"We could put him in jail," I suggest softly.

"Sure, but then I risk hurting my mother even more. I would need to pay someone to take care of her, and I can't afford that. I could take care of her myself, but I'd need to get a bigger place to live, and I can't afford that either. She also has no friends, so she would be completely alone without my father."

"I see." My first instinct is to offer some of my family's money, but I know Liam is too prideful to accept it and will just get angry at me. His nightmares make me concerned. I vaguely remember learning in school that dreams can have great significance to our mental health. I have been worrying that Liam hasn't been getting enough sleep lately; he's been working himself to the bone, and even when he is at home, he's been avoiding coming to bed. Is it because of this nightmare?

I clear my throat. "Have you considered seeing a therapist to find out what the dream means?"

Liam curses under his breath. "I don't need a fucking shrink, Helen. I need to go to work. I'm running late."

With that, he turns and leaves, and I find myself frowning at his harsh manner. This isn't the Liam I know and love. What has gotten into him? I thought we were in a good place, and it's painful to think he was hiding this from me all along. Maybe he's right. It *is* for the best that I'm not pregnant if he has some deep-seated family drama to work through. We can't be ready for new life, and new family, unless we can heal our relationships with our existing family.

Unfortunately, we're going to have to sort out our communication issues fast, and figure out whatever's bothering him before our wedding. I don't want to walk down the aisle with him unless our minds are clear and our hearts are open. But can we overcome his lifelong nightmare in two weeks? I hope so.

We have already bought our tickets to Paris, and I have been looking forward to the adventure of a lifetime with the love of my life.

Chapter Two

"Is there something wrong with me?" I ask my doctor nervously.

"No," Leslie says with a smile. "Even for a perfectly healthy woman, it can take a while to get pregnant. There are so many factors that come into play. Don't worry so much, and just keep trying! Stressing about it will only make it more challenging."

"But my periods are so irregular," I tell her with a frown.

"Have you been tracking how often you get them?" she asks me.

"Only recently. It's been something like every 38 to 45 days."

"That could still be normal," Dr. Leslie Howard says while making notes. It's strange seeing her like this now, in a lab coat. I haven't visited her office for a while, since she's usually been present at family gatherings for the past few months. "Having a cycle that's a little longer than the average is still healthy, as long as it's fairly regular. Have you missed any periods altogether?"

"Yes. Earlier this year when I was in that car crash."

"Have you ever missed multiple periods in a row?" she asks.

I shake my head. "No. I don't think so. But... I was blind for quite a while, so it's hard to say for sure. I used to start wearing pads as soon as I started to feel cramps or breast tenderness, a few days before I expected my period. I also wore the pads a day or two after I stopped feeling that sticky wetness, just to be sure." Hesitating, I think back farther and begin to worry. Sometimes it's hard to remember what life was like before I could see. How did I get by at all? How did I live each day, not knowing all these basic things, like whether there was blood staining my underwear?

"Were your periods heavy or painful?" she asks.

"Not really. Sometimes I had very light periods," I explain, "with no pain to warn me that they were coming. That happened a lot when I was living on my own in New Hampshire, and I guess... I can't really be sure if I got my period at all. When I was away, I couldn't ask Carmen to check and see if I was bleeding—sometimes it just feels the same as, you know, being turned on."

Leslie nods and jots down more information. I suddenly feel very awkward and embarrassed talking about this, because I remember that Leslie is now *dating my father*. A hot blush reaches my cheeks, and I don't need to be able to see to confirm that my cheeks are actually bright red. I just talked to my father's girlfriend about being turned on. And she nodded. Does that mean that she has been turned on lately? By my dad? This is just way too weird.

I am lucky that she does not even notice the topic, and continues to discuss my health. "When you came back from New Hampshire, you were very underweight. While you weren't malnourished, simply being underweight can result in hormonal changes and missed periods. It's called amenorrhea. Going forward, now that you can see, I want you to pay more attention to your periods and write down when you get them. Also, if you notice any pain during ovulation, around the middle of your period, make note of when that happens, too."

"Okay," I say, as my worries return. *What if there really is something wrong?*

"Amenorrhea occurs often in female athletes with low body fat percentages," she explains. "You're still pretty skinny, so I would recommend that you make sure you're getting enough calories every day. You should aim for 2000 calories, especially once you get pregnant. Also, keep taking those prenatal vitamins and DHA—maybe even set an alarm so you don't forget to take them. Oh, and Helen? You might want to cut back on the wine."

I feel my shoulders sloop in sheepish guilt. "I'll try."

"Don't try," she says firmly. "It's necessary that you make all the lifestyle changes you need to make *now*, so your body is strong *before* going into the pregnancy. So many women just flip a switch and decide to be health-conscious once they've conceived, but it's already too late. Your body is still recovering from the damage you were doing to it before, on a regular basis. That means your body is wasting precious resources fixing itself instead of nourishing the embryo during critical stages of development."

I gulp at the harsh, didactic tone in her voice. She sounds like a teacher who was disappointed in my assignment because she thinks I can do so much better. She sounds like an employer who is disappointed in my work performance, and would really like to promote me if I'd just bring my A-game. She sounds like… a parent.

"Besides," Leslie says a little more gently, "changing habits is a massive undertaking. With the amount of wine you drink, you probably have some dependency issues. You'll have to cut back slowly to avoid any unsavory withdrawal symptoms, like headaches, shaky hands, or insomnia."

"Leslie!" I say with wide eyes. "Are you calling me an alcoholic?"

"No. I said nothing of the sort."

"But you and Dad went to wine country this weekend and came home with *five cases* of vintage wine!" I say accusingly. "You encouraged me to try a little from each vineyard!"

"That was done strictly as a friend, and now I'm speaking as your doctor."

"It's not fair," I tell her. "Maybe you could set a good example by not drinking so much in front of me. It doesn't make it easier."

"Honey, when you've gone through menopause, you can have all the wine you want. Personally, I reserve the right to have a few glasses and enjoy my old age with that dashing grey gentleman..."

"Too much information!" I say quickly, trying to avoid the imagery of Dad and Leslie getting it on.

Leslie laughs lightly. "Okay, we'll try to tone it down a little when you come by my house."

Her house. The reminder that our house was partially destroyed in a fire sobers me up a little. It's hard to believe that Grayson's best friend was far crazier than he was and would go to such lengths to hurt my sister. It's been several months, and insurance did pay for the repairs, but the house still isn't ready for us to move back in. I've been mostly staying at Liam's, while Dad stays with Leslie, and Carmen stays alone in her new penthouse apartment. With the house gone, we've all been separated again.

Thinking about what Carmen's been through lately brings me back to my original goal.

A baby.

"Are there any tests I can do to make sure I'm fertile?" I ask Dr. Howard. "I read about AMH testing to see how many eggs I have remaining. What about Liam's sperm count? Do you think it would be helpful to have him tested? What about

DNA testing us both to make sure the baby won't have any birth defects or abnormalities..."

"Helen!" Leslie exclaims. "Calm down. All of that is completely unnecessary."

"But Carmen lost her baby," I say in a hoarse voice. "I know that Brad drugged her, but is it possible that there was something about the baby that made it unhealthy? Something genetic, something to do with our family?"

"It's unlikely," Leslie says in a soft voice. "Carmen's baby was healthy, Helen. It was your sister who was unable to carry to full term, for a variety of reasons, physical and emotional. Stress plays a very important role."

I nod slowly. "Still—if there are any tests I can do at all—just to make sure things will go well. I would like to just... know something."

Leslie hesitates. She turns around and goes to her desk in the examination room. She ruffles through some papers for a moment, but not finding what she is looking for, pulls her phone out of her pocket. She scans through something with her thumb, and I grow anxious wondering whether she's reading notes, emails, or text messages. I hold my breath, anticipating bad news.

"You know, genetic testing might be a good idea," Leslie says finally, "or more specifically, genetic counseling for you two as a couple. I can get you into a clinical trial being conducted by some of my colleagues at John's Hopkins. After all, we do know that you are a carrier of LCA, and it might be useful to know if Liam is also a carrier. It is an autosomal recessive disease, which would give your children a 25% chance of being born blind if he is a carrier. But in some rare cases, your disease may be dominant, and your child could have an increased risk of being born with LCA."

I take a deep breath. My whole life, I've been aware that there was a chance that my children could also be born blind. There were times when I thought it was better to give up any hope of having kids, but those days are long behind me. "While that's scary, it's not my biggest concern. My quality of life wasn't hugely impacted by my blindness. I just want to know if I'll have a healthy baby... who survives."

"Then take advantage of this study," Leslie says softly. "LCA is your way in, but they will thoroughly test both you and Liam for all possible genetic abnormalities. They work fast, too. All you have to do is send in sealed vials of your saliva, and then you'll be able to view your information online. You can also meet with a counselor if you need more advice. The study is about the impact of genetic knowledge on couples trying to conceive, so you will have to agree to fill out questionnaires about the experience, and all the information will remain confidential."

I stare at her for a moment as I ponder this. "I am not sure that Liam will like the idea."

"For good reason," Leslie says. "It could open a world of information that you'd be better off not finding out. Sometimes couples get so scared that they decide not to have a baby at all to avoid the risk of having a sick child, when in reality, their child might have been perfectly healthy. This information can destroy relationships."

I am having trouble prioritizing Liam over the health of my potential children. "Would you do it if you were in my shoes, Leslie?"

"Absolutely. Having a healthy baby is like winning the genetic lottery. Before diving in, a DNA test could help you understand the odds of the game a little better. Just don't get discouraged and stop trying, because if you don't buy a ticket, you can't win."

My shoulders relax and a smile settles on my face. "Okay. Sign me up!"

"I'll email you the information," Leslie says. "Usually, I would only recommend the testing for a couple who already had a child born with a defect or chromosomal abnormality, but I consider you family, Helen. It's better to be safe than sorry. Any amount of information you can gather beforehand could give you the ability to anticipate and treat problems before they even arise."

"You don't have to sell me any more on this. The last time you sent a medical study my way, gene therapy cured my eyes and landed me a fiancé. It couldn't hurt to give this one a try."

"Just give it some serious thought first, Helen." She pauses and looks at me sympathetically. "Everyone has the potential for all kinds of horrible, unwanted diseases programmed into their DNA. You might go in looking to ease your mind, and it might give you all kinds of additional stress you don't need. When you're dealing with genetics, you never know what kind of frightening information you might discover."

The tone of her voice gives me a chill. "Maybe I'll discover that I have latent superpowers?" I say hopefully.

Leslie doesn't smile. "Be careful what you wish for."

Chapter Three

Dr. Liam Larson

"For the last time, Owen. I will *not* do a Magic Mike dance routine with you at my wedding."

"Why not?" Owen says with a pout.

"Because it's not going to be that kind of wedding," I explain. "It's going to be simple and low-key."

"You're boring," Owen grumbles between sips of his appletini. Yes, he actually ordered an appletini. At a sports bar. "Can we perform any dance routine at all?" he pleads.

"No."

"Fine," Owen says, sulking and nursing his bright green cocktail. "You'll never go viral on YouTube with that attitude."

I fight back a smile. I don't know why anything about him surprises me anymore. Lately, we've been lucky enough to have some shifts at work that finish around the same time, so we've been trying to uphold the time-honored manly tradition of having a drink after work. But while most of the men around us are 'having beer with the guys' in the true American fashion, Owen feels the constant need to thwart social convention and confuse everyone by ordering girly drinks or colorful margaritas roughly the size of his own head. Owen is simply Owen, I wouldn't have him any other way.

"So how small is this wedding going to be?" he asks me.

Taking a swig of my scotch, I lean back in my chair. "We've narrowed it down to eight people."

"Eight people!" he exclaims in horror. "Liam, are you crazy? I'm almost surprised that you have room for me! Are you even inviting anyone from work?"

"No. I don't want to involve them in my personal life."

"Earth to Liam! Have you gone and become a minimalist monk when I wasn't looking? Jesus! If you're scared of doing seating plans, I can help," Owen offers. "Isn't that what the best man is for? I can cross-reference your guests with Helen's and make sure that no one wants to murder their dinner companions. It took me and Caroline a whole week to get our seating plan right."

"For the wedding that you didn't actually go through with?" I remind him dryly. "You're hardly the expert, buddy. The whole point is to actually *get married*."

"That's not the point at all! The point is to *celebrate.* My non-wedding was still a great party; everyone had fun and danced, even if no one actually got married. Isn't that better than a stiff, cold, mechanical signing of papers in a courtroom?"

"Well, it's not going to be that basic. We're going to have flowers and some friends and family, and a nice dinner. It's going to be sweet and memorable, but we are saving our money and our focus for having an actual successful *marriage,* not just an extravagant wedding to show off and compensate for our insecurities about our relationship."

"Hey," Owen says with a bit of hurt in his voice. "Caroline's dad forced me into that whole thing. I would have gone through with the wedding if Caroline didn't want to go off and find herself."

"I know," I say apologetically, "but it really was the best thing for you in the end."

"It was," Owen says softly. "Things have been so easy since I began dating Carmen. Love is supposed to be easy, isn't it? You're supposed to want the same things. Life with someone you care about shouldn't be a constant game of tug-o-war."

"Yeah," I say softly, taking another long drink. I feel guilty for running out on Helen this morning, but these nightmares have been leaving me really shaken up. Even during my lunch break today, when I crashed for a few minutes in the break room, I somehow had the same damned dream. Always my mother, always that baby. If I could somehow avoid going to sleep at all, I would.

"Caroline has been doing really well since our non-wedding," Owen tells me. "She's wild and free and happy, and experimenting with dating lots of incredibly hot women. We stay in touch, and she sends me pics. That was my one condition in accepting her becoming a lesbian and leaving me at the altar—there must be hot pics. I honestly think she's gotten more action in the past three months than I have in my entire life."

"Who's getting action?" A female voice interrupts our conversation.

I look up to see that Helen is approaching our table, and a smile brightens my face. I stand up to give her a hug and a kiss on the cheek before making room for her in our booth. She slides in to sit beside me and places a hand on my leg as she looks up at me with a bit of sadness in her dark eyes. Her eyes have always been a landscape of emotion, fast-changing and breathtaking; I pride myself on being able to discern her thoughts and feelings from their shadows and shine, long before she ever speaks. After all, I have operated on those eyes multiple times, and none should be more acquainted with them than I am. Now, it is easy to decipher that she is disappointed and worried, and once again, I feel guilty for the way I left things this morning.

"We were just talking about my ex," Owen says cheerfully. "She's having so much fun since she gave up on men and chose scissors over forks."

"I don't see how any of the women in your life could *not* want to give up on men and become lesbians," my fiancée says, and a wicked glint enters her eyes as her lips curl in a tiny smirk.

"Ouch," Owen says, clutching his heart. "I fear that may be true, good lady."

Helen nods gravely. "Speaking of another soon-to-be-lesbian, where is my sister? I thought you were going to convince her to join us?"

"She doesn't feel like leaving her penthouse," Owen says with a shrug. "Since the event, she's locked herself up there like a princess in a tower. I'm just lucky that she lets me climb up her hair now and then."

Helen is quiet for a moment as she reaches out to grasp my scotch. The glass is nearly to her lips when she hesitates and stares down at the amber liquid pensively.

Reaching to my side, I place my hand on the small of her back. She continues to stare at my drink, and I feel the need to interrupt her reverie. "How was your day?" I ask her as I run my hand over her back. "How's the book coming along?"

She glances at me and sighs as she places my drink down and pushes it around on the table. "I couldn't write because I was so stressed out. I went to see Dr. Howard, and she confirmed that I'm *still* not pregnant—but she did give me some interesting advice about the whole situation."

"What advice?" I ask her, but the feelings of dread begin to return at the mention of pregnancy.

The images from my nightmare return, and I feel a little sick at the realistic sensation of holding the bloody newborn in my arms. I never had much of a creative streak, but being engaged to a writer must be rubbing off on me—my imagination is going wild.

"Dr. Howard was telling me—"

Owen cuts in before she can finish: "Helen, I want to apologize on behalf of Liam's swimmers. They are clearly an inexperienced and disorganized bunch of soldiers. If you need a real man to get up in there and impreg…"

"No," I say in unison with Helen who makes a face as she nearly shouts, *"No!"*

"What?" Owen asks innocently. "I was going to say that I have a great OBGYN friend who could help with IVF or something like that."

Helen rolls her eyes at this. I am about to roast my buddy for doubting my swimmers, but the waitress comes around at this moment with our order of appetizers. She expertly balances all the plates before placing them down on the center of the table. My mouth begins to water at the sight of sliders, mozzarella sticks, and my personal favorite, chicken wings. The perfect comfort food after a long day at work. As soon as the waitress leaves, everyone reaches for a wing.

I am so eager to take my first bite that I rip into the meat without thinking. As soon as the sauce hits my tongue, my eyes begin to water. When I inhale sharply, I swear that my nostril hairs are singeing due to the insane amount of heat on this tiny wing.

"Owen!" I manage to croak out between fits of coughing. "What the hell did you order?" It takes great strength to fight back the urge to throttle him, but then again, it usually does. Looking over to my left, I see that Helen is also surprised by the heat, but handling it far better than I am. Her eyebrows are lifted in amusement, but she doesn't seem too enraged, and she isn't even reaching for a glass of water.

"It's the Triple Homicide Hellfire," Owen boasts proudly. "You were in the bathroom, so I decided to be creative. Plus, there's three of us. I thought it was poetic."

"But then," Helen says as she licks the sauce off her fingers, "wouldn't it be murder-suicide?"

"No way!" Owen says sharply, ripping a chunk of meat off with his teeth, caveman-style. His eyes begin to tear up and his face grows red as he speaks haltingly. "Everyone knows suicide wings are for pussies. Triple Homicide Hellfire is the sauce of real men."

"Owen, you're crying like a baby," I point out. "Maybe you should have ordered the sauce of lesser men."

"Oh, Liam, my dear and delusional friend," Owen says, shaking his head slowly as tears slide down his cheeks. "Don't you know anything? Chicken wings are like sex. If it's not hot enough to make you cry, you're not doing it right. And you're never going to get anyone pregnant with that attitude!"

Helen and I stare at him for a moment in astonishment, until I hear her begin to laugh softly beside me.

I nudge her with my knee. "Hey, don't take him seriously. I'm totally doing it right."

"You are," she says softly, "usually. But it didn't seem like you were making enough time this past month, to actually try."

She is right, of course. Around her ovulation when we both knew that she was most fertile, I somehow managed to pick up extra shifts at work and barely be home at all. What is wrong with me? We decided to do this together. I legitimately tried my best to get her pregnant in previous months, but lately I've been losing focus and growing distant. Why am I avoiding her? Why am I so freaked out that I can't even think about having a child without feeling like I'm going to vomit?

"I've been wondering if you changed your mind about wanting kids," Helen is saying hesitantly. "It just doesn't really feel like you're all-in."

"There's your problem right there," Owen says, leaning forward with an ear-to-ear grin. "It definitely has to feel like he's all in."

Helen glares at him and Owen makes a high-pitched yelp.

"Ow! Wha'd'you that for?" he mumbles, and I gather that she kicked him under the table.

"But it could be pointless," Helen says, ignoring Owen and turning to me. "Even if we had more time to try… there could just be something wrong with me."

A pang of fear causes my chest to tighten. "What do you mean?"

"Leslie said that I might have amenorrhea due to being underweight. I might not be able to conceive unless I get healthier and my hormones are more balanced."

"I see," I say quietly, but it feels like a weight has been lifted from my shoulders. What the hell is wrong with me? I know that I want to have children, so why have I been so scared shitless lately? What is up with this gnawing feeling in my gut that something is going to go wrong? Nothing can go wrong. Helen and I are happy together, and we're as ready as we're ever going to be. All the pain and complications that we suffered through when we first met is far behind us. Why can't I let go and move forward?

"Waitress!" Owen shouts out loudly as he flags down our server. "Get this woman a plate of nachos. She's trying to have a baby!"

When the whole bar erupts in cheers and applause, and dozens of strange men lift their beers in congratulations, I know that I should be enjoying this moment a whole lot more. I force a smile and give a small wave of thanks to calm them all down.

Helen's cheeks darken considerably. "God, Owen. Why don't you give every Yankees fan in the city front row seats to our bedroom while you're at it?!"

"You're joking, right?" Owen asks. "Of course, you're joking! But wait—are you joking? Because I could get a lot of money for…"

"She's joking," I tell Owen, reaching forward to steal his drink. "You're gonna have to lay off the appletinis, buddy."

As he sulks, I turn my attention back to Helen. Her eyes are downcast, and I can see that she is genuinely worried about her ability to get pregnant. I feel responsible for taking care of her emotions and her health, and I know how important this is to her. When we first got engaged and started trying to conceive, we were both so happy and filled with hope for the future. I don't know what changed along the way, but my anxiety has been building to the point where I sometimes want to run away and hide in my car, and blast music loud enough to split my eardrums.

I realize that Helen and Owen have been chatting while I've been lost inside my own head, and I try to tune in to their conversation.

"…really only inviting eight people?" Owen is asking, incredulous.

"Eight?" Helen responds, looking to me with puzzlement. "Liam, I know we agreed on a small wedding, but we can't possibly trim the list down anymore. Didn't we agree on ten people?"

"Yeah," I say hesitantly, "but I'm not comfortable with inviting my mother and father."

Helen and Owen exchange looks.

"You have to, bro," Owen says gently, wiping the hellfire sauce off his lips with a napkin. "You'll regret it if you don't. Besides, haven't you started trying to mend your relationship with your mother? She'll be so brokenhearted if she doesn't get to come to the wedding of *her only child*."

A little shiver runs through my spine as I remember my dream. I toss the rest of my scotch down my throat before reaching for Owen's appletini. I finish off his beverage in the space of a millisecond, and I am surprised to note that the flavor was quite refreshing, and not sickly sweet like I had imagined. I'll never admit it to him, or anyone, but I really liked that damn appletini, and I almost want to order another for myself.

"Liam," Helen says, placing gentle pressure on my leg with her small hand. "I thought things were getting better with your mother?"

"Kind of," I tell her softly, grasping her hand in mine and interlacing my fingers with hers. "I don't mind my mother so much, but every time I go to pick her up, I see my father staring at me from the window with these demon-eyes. He looks like he's formulating a plan to peel my skin off and bury me alive, or maybe just hoping that I'll burn in hell."

Helen shudders a little. "Do you really think he means you harm? Even so, what could he do from the confines of a wheelchair?"

"He can do enough," I inform her. "He can do

more than enough."

"I understand you not inviting your father," Owen tells me, leaning forward with a frown. "After all, you are inviting James, right? You can substitute a judo master for a father—that's what happens in all the cool martial arts movies! But you really should let your mom come, Liam. She's just as much a victim as you are."

Inhaling deeply, I find myself frowning. "Is she?"

"Ow," Helen says, pulling her hand away. Only then do I realize that my grip had tightened to the point where I was crushing her. "Are you okay?" she asks me with a startled look.

"Yeah," I say, exhaling deeply. "I just don't like thinking about my family and the way I grew up. It makes me miserable and keeps me up at night."

"That's not good," Owen says. "You're going to need your beauty sleep before the wedding! Those photos will be hanging on the walls for your kids and grandkids to see, for generations and generations. It simply won't do if you have gross puffy bags under your eyes, Liam."

"Great," I say glumly, "now I feel even worse. Can someone please change the subject?"

Helen nods. "Actually, there is something I wanted to discuss," she says slowly and with a bit of excitement in her voice. "How do you feel about genetic counseling?"

I look at her with surprise. "You mean DNA

testing a couple trying to conceive? But isn't that for people who think they might be carriers of something like Huntington's disease or Tay-Sachs?"

"Usually, but Leslie said that we could get into the study because of my LCA." Helen pauses and glances at me furtively. "Besides, we might be carriers of those diseases and not even know it. I think it would be really reassuring to find out, Liam."

Her reasoning is solid. As a doctor, I spend so much time thinking about the health of others that I have never really considered genetic testing for myself. The dark pit in my chest opens wider, as more and more fear accumulates inside me. What am I afraid of? Genetic testing could be a great idea, right? But what if we found some hidden disaster, buried deep in our DNA. What if we learned that our child could be born with some incapacitating illness, like cystic fibrosis, or worse yet, some rare disease that doesn't even allow the baby to live until its first birthday?

It's rare, but it happens. As many patients as I see due to accidents or lack of maintenance, a large portion of the sick people are still visiting the hospital due to issues that they were born with—like Helen.

The results can't possibly be good. That's the problem with genetic testing: they will *always* discover things that are wrong with you. Our DNA holds the secrets to all the ticking time bombs that will eventually explode, with devastating consequences to our bodies and our lives. While I am not a geneticist, I have some idea of the nastiness that we could discover. Will I get dementia or Alzheimer's when I'm older, and lose my mind? Do I have an extremely high risk of getting a certain type of cancer? These are just some of the things that quickly come to mind. If we have children, will they be doomed to suffer all the pain that we have felt, in addition to all the pain we narrowly escaped by not having *all* the bad genes required for a certain disease?

And worse yet, how have our lives impacted our genetic material? Have I had too much to drink, have I spent too much time in the sun, have I been around too many chemicals? What mutations have occurred, and what darkness will we pass down that cannot be measured? Will I be a good father? Will I even be an *adequate* father? Will I be there enough? Will *I* be enough?

Or will I be a monster? Cruel and full of hatred, like my father?

And will my sons have to suffer for my sins?

"Hey," Helen says, rubbing my arm. "Liam? Do you think it's a good idea?"

I gaze at her, and study her features. It's hard to believe that she is mine. This beautiful, strong, funny, and impossibly independent woman is going to be my wife. *My actual wife.* It feels like my brain and body are still caught somewhere in the past, and struggling to catch up to my reality. We're happy.

Loretta Lost

We're going to continue being happy. We're safe from harm, and financially secure. We respect each other. All these good things surround me, so why do I feel so... cold?

There is no baby. There never was a baby.

The words echo in my brain, and I wonder what they mean. Will we learn that having children together will result in heartache? Will she leave me? Sometimes I don't understand why she sticks around anyway, after all that I've done. After all the lies, and after seeing my family—surely she must know that there are many men out there who would be a far better choice for her to marry. Other men, in her social class, might not have to work so hard to become successful. They could spend more time at home, more time with her, and more time with any children they might have.

"Be careful, Helen," Owen says as he polishes off the mozzarella sticks. "He has his serious-thinking face on. Whatever's going on in his head is dark and heavy. We may even be in for a lecture."

I swallow a bit of saliva before shaking my head. "No lecture. I just don't think DNA testing is right for us. There are privacy concerns, for starters; it is such a new field that there aren't enough laws in place to protect our genetic information. Insurance companies could take advantage of the reports and decide to decline coverage, or increase the rates until they are astronomically high."

"See?" Owen says. "He's lecturing."

Helen shakes her head. "I don't care about

insurance, Liam. Maybe we can do the tests anonymously, or under pseudonyms. What does privacy matter when we're thinking about the health of our future children?"

"There's nothing we can do with the information," I tell her. "So what, we take the tests and find out something really fucked up—are we just going to decide we don't want children? Are we going to break up and go find other people to have children with, so they won't be sick? Or are we going to gamble?"

"Liam, this isn't fair," Helen says quietly. "I just… I don't want what happened to Carmen to happen to me."

Her features are darkened by grief and uneasiness. When I turn to Owen for help, I see that he has a similar look on his face. I know that Carmen losing her baby really affected both of them, and Owen has been working tirelessly to help find a solution to her infertility.

"I think you should do it," Owen tells me earnestly, before taking a bite out of a homicidal chicken wing. When his eyes grow teary, I know he is trying to dissolve the tension of the serious situation with comedy. "Genetic counseling is a great idea, and this sounds like a wonderful opportunity."

"Maybe," I say, pulling out my wallet and placing a few bills on the table. "But this is between me and Helen, and our DNA, so I think we're going to have to discuss the situation in private."

"That's not nice," Owen says with a pout. "We're practically family!"

Rising to my feet, I place a hand on his shoulder. "I know, brother. If you ask me, DNA is bullshit. The whole concept of blood relatives is bullshit. You are the family I choose, and I would lay down my life for you. I never had much luck with the other kind. No one who was actually blood ever bothered to give a shit. My parents hate my guts. My father considered me a nuisance to avoid from the moment I was born. Why would my children be any different?"

"They would be," Helen says softly. "Your children will adore you, Liam. They will idolize you, and you will be their hero. Because you're everything that a good father should be. You're the man that your father should have been."

Her words cause my heart to swell. The darkness inside me recedes a little, and I feel stronger. Is it true? Does she mean it?

Placing her hand on my arm, Helen smiles at me. "I'm sorry that you never got to experience what a real father is like, but you will now. My father will be there for us, and he'll teach us all the things that we need to know."

I frown a little. "Your dad nearly broke us up…"

"He may have been a real asshole to you this past year, but he has always kept our best interests at heart. I think he was mostly just testing us. He did help us out financially, and help with your career, after all. He's a *good* father, and he will be a *great* grandfather."

"Hey," Owen says, rising to his feet and looping one arm around me, and the other around Helen. "You guys are so gloomy. Who cares about all this ancient history? One or two bad apples in your immediate family isn't the end of the world. Our lives are made up of all the interactions with the dozens of people we meet along the way: teachers, friends, colleagues, lovers, strangers on the bus, dental hygienists, and parole officers."

"And the books we read," Helen adds as she makes eye contact with me. "The TV shows and movies that we watch."

"Yeah!" Owen says, clapping me on the back. "We're all related somehow. Just by spending time with each other, and communicating like this, we are affected; we are changed. Cheer up, Liam. Maybe your kids will be the first members of your bloodline you'll really be proud to call family."

"Maybe," I say quietly, but I can't shake the feeling that something is wrong.

There is no baby. There never was a baby.

These words send a chill through me, like a supernatural omen forewarning of disaster. Somehow, I don't think I'll ever have a son or daughter to hold in my arms.

Chapter Four

Helen Winters

"I won't do it, Helen."

"Please," I implore him, "try to be reasonable about this."

Liam shakes his head as he moves around the apartment. "I already told you my reasons. The genetic counseling is a bad idea, and I don't want to get tested. If you want to get tested on your own, I completely understand, but it's a personal choice."

"It's not *that* personal. I am not the only one contributing genetic material to the baby."

"Jesus, Helen, please! Can we stop talking about the baby stuff for five minutes? I just want to relax right now. I need to relax." Walking over to the couch, Liam pulls off his shirt before collapsing to the cushions.

My eyebrows furrow as I look at the limp man in the couch. Something seems really off about

Liam. I feel puzzled as I walk over and kneel beside him. I study his face and body, and a thought occurs to me. "Liam, have you lost weight?" I ask. He looks a lot leaner than he did a few months ago at my cabin in Pennsylvania.

"Yeah," he says tiredly as he runs the back of his hand across his eyes. "Just about fifteen pounds or so. I haven't had as much time to work out lately."

I place a hand on his muscled shoulder, and I realize that I can feel the difference in his physique. How did I not notice before? I'm not the only one with a low body-fat percentage. Are his dreams really so bad that they are taking a physical toll on him? If so, I should really try to get him help, but I don't know how I could do it in a way that doesn't make him upset. I try to remember his recent dietary habits: obviously, I'm not the best cook, and we get a lot of takeout food. But I haven't even seen Liam eating much of that—he mainly seems to subsist on coffee and five-hour energy drinks.

"Liam?" I say softly, with mounting apprehension. "Do you need to see a doctor?"

He groans, turning away from me slightly in the couch. "It's just these damn nightmares. They won't let me sleep."

"The dream about the baby?"

"Yes. I'm sorry, Helen. The pressure is really getting to me. With how much time I spend at work, and now with my mother... I just keep thinking that I'm going to fail as a parent. Maybe we should revisit the idea in a few months, or years, maybe after I've established my private practice and feel a little more comfortable in my career."

"I... I don't know," I tell him softly, dropping to a cross-legged sitting position on the floor. "I'm scared, too, Liam. But I really think that we should do it. It will only get more physically challenging for me to get pregnant and give birth as I get older. Plus, we will have less time to spend with our children, the older we are before having them. We will miss more of their lives."

"Are you sure this isn't just about Carmen?" he asks. "Do you just feel sorry for your sister and want to make up for the loss somehow?"

"For god's sake, Liam! I want this. I thought you wanted this, too." I sigh. "It isn't just about Carmen. Of course, what happened to her factors into this. But everyone in my life factors into this. I'm the only person capable of having children in my family, or in our little circle. Dad and Leslie can't have kids. Owen and Carmen might never be able to. I feel a kind of... responsibility."

"Those are bad reasons," Liam tells me. "Family isn't the way it used to be. If you have a child, it's not going to matter that much to anyone else. You think that it will—but look at how many years you spent alone. In this city, people are always alone and isolated. You think the child would grow up with a doting grandfather and grandmother, or a cheerful aunt and uncle to take them to movies, or skating, or to the park. But those

44

people might not be happy for you. They might desert you, or be jealous. What if Carmen's reaction isn't to love our child and be its favorite auntie, but she becomes the bitter old maid who is jealous that you had what she couldn't?"

"No," I say in surprise. "She isn't like that."

"She could be. You never know how people will react. Also, people get divorced, Helen. What happens if our differences break us apart, and we end up going our separate ways? What if I end up seeing the kids only on weekends and holidays?"

"Don't even talk like that," I tell him sharply, and I find myself fighting back tears. "Why are you being so negative?"

"I'm being realistic and talking about all the possible outcomes. DNA is the least of our concerns. Parents do so much emotional damage to their children that it overshadows any physical harm that could be caused by an unlucky genetic matchup."

"Then why do you even want to get married to me?" I ask him. "Do you want to back out of that, too? If so many things can go wrong and we are doomed to failure, then why bother trying?"

Liam sighs. "We're not doomed to failure, Helen. I just have a headache, and I'm not feeling very well right now."

"I don't understand you," I tell him harshly, standing up and moving away. "You've always been so brave and determined, and right now you're just being weak."

"Why is it weak to question our decision? I just don't think there are any good reasons to rush to have children right now. Can you think of one good reason?"

"I have a thousand reasons. But mainly, I love you and I think this would bring us joy and make us feel more fulfilled."

He pauses for a few minutes before responding, and my anxiety grows as I wait for him to answer. I am beginning to think he has fallen asleep when he finally speaks again. "I think I was wrong," he says. "I think I was just swept away in the excitement of getting engaged, and that I'm not really ready to start a family. People are having children at much older ages these days. Maybe we can wait."

I put my hands up in the air in surrender. "Sure, Liam. Do you want to cancel the wedding, too? Were you just swept up in the excitement of saving me from a car accident and performing surgery on me, so you felt like a hero? But you didn't really want to be stuck with me for the long term after all?"

"You're being overemotional right now, Helen. Of course, I still want to marry you, you foolish woman. I think we both need to get some sleep."

"Fine," I tell him in annoyance, moving toward the bedroom. "But you can sleep right there. We don't want to risk you getting me pregnant!"

He turns over in the couch to face me, and I

can see the dark shadows under his eyes. He forces a little smile. "Maybe we can risk it sometime soon, when I'm feeling a bit better."

It's hard to see him like this. I don't really know what to do. "Hey," I say softly. "Can we please do the DNA testing anyway? I still think we should find out what information we can, even if we decide to delay having children."

"No," he says, turning away again. "I won't do it. But feel free to get tested without me."

"I will," I tell him, moving toward the bedroom. I am very frustrated as I reach for my phone and text Leslie:

> Is it possible for me to get the genetic counseling alone? Liam doesn't want to participate, but I really do.

Delivered

I wait for a few seconds before my phone pings.

Sorry, Helen. They won't allow that since the study is about couples.

My stomach sinks a little and I feel crushed. I was unable to see for so long, and I hate being in the dark about anything at all; literally or figuratively. I am staring blankly at the walls and feeling sorry for myself when my phone pings again.

I called Dr. Nguyen and he said that they were closed to new applications, but I convinced him to open up a spot. He agreed to test you and Liam, as long as you collect the samples ASAP and overnight FedEx them to his office. If you are trying to make Liam change his mind, you only have a few hours. You could come to my office and do it tomorrow, or I could give you the vials and you could collect the saliva on your own.

Loretta Lost

Collect the saliva on my own? A terrible idea strikes me, and I move back to the doorway of the bedroom to gaze upon Liam's sleeping form. I wonder how difficult it would be to steal his saliva? Should I try to do it now? Would I have to keep it cold, or is it different from harvesting an organ? Not that I know much about harvesting organs, but I have seen movies.

Oh god, is this a crime? It must be an invasion of privacy or something of the sort. It really is cruel of me to even consider stealing my fiancé's genetic material so that I can get information to make myself feel better. But maybe if I'm careful, I could conceal my actions so that he never finds out? I could use fake names to protect our privacy, and I could make sure that no one has access to his information other than me.

It can't do any harm, right? He was just so adamantly against the idea, but what if he changes his mind at some point in the future? We could probably get tested from a different source, but it would take forever. With us getting married in two weeks, and with the potential of having children together...

I need to know.

The guilt I feel is dwarfed by my curiosity and need for reassurance. I lift my phone to text Dr. Howard back:

> I will come by and pick up the vials from you tomorrow. Thanks, Leslie! 😊

Delivered

Somehow, I already feel better. I feel like a spy, or a secret agent. I feel like a badass, like we are Mr. and Mrs. Smith about to double cross each other, but only to be clever and gain the upper hand—not to actually hurt each other. Moving over to the bed, I formulate my plan of attack. How will I steal Liam's saliva without him noticing? And how much do I need? I will need to ask Leslie tomorrow. She said that it needed to be collected in a vial, so it probably is a little more than a quick swab.

Liam will need to be more than just deeply asleep. He'll need to lose consciousness.

An idea suddenly strikes me.

Yes. It's perfect.

Tightening my grip on my phone, I scroll through my contacts and find the person I need to dial. When I hear the voice on the other end of the line, I smirk to myself.

"I need your help," I say in a whisper, so Liam cannot hear me. "I need you to steal something for me."

There is silence, and then a voice speaks:

"Why should I help you?"

"Because," I demand in a hushed voice, "you owe me."

Chapter Five

As I exit Dr. Howard's office with the vials and instructions tucked away in my purse, I begin feeling like a sexy secret agent again. When the sun hits my face and I have to reach up and pull my sunglasses down to protect my eyes, I legitimately feel like a superhero. Being able to see so much brightness that I need to dim my vision is still so novel to me.

Heading over to my new car, I open up the driver's door and slide into the seat. A familiar pang of pain in my abdomen causes me to wince. Of course—I got my period earlier today. I didn't really need to head to the doctor to confirm that I wasn't pregnant yesterday, because if I had just been patient, I would have had my answer today. However, I am happy to see my period, because I know that it is a sign that I am healthy.

To combat the menstrual cramps, I turn on the heated seats of my new Toyota before putting the car in gear to drive to my destination. I discovered last month, very much by accident, that the heated seats feel wonderful on my lower back and just completely soothe the pain.

Anyway, I won't allow mundane menstrual cramps to interfere with my exciting secret mission. No real lady spy ever would. Not that I know much about real lady spies, but I have seen movies. I think that if I could have any career other than being a writer, I would definitely want to be a spy. Writing was always my dream job when I was growing up, but after I've actually written a few books and experienced the soul-crushing immobility of sitting at a desk for hundreds of hours, I can't help fantasizing about something more exciting. Something where I get to move around.

Although writing may be the most adventurous job imaginable when it comes to the mind, it is one of the most isolating and uninteresting jobs when it comes to the body. I sometimes look back on my time spent locked away in my cabin in New Hampshire, and I wonder what on earth I was thinking. Being so cooped up, never touching another human being, and hardly even hearing other human voices—it really was self-inflicted torture.

I think that part of me was dying a little on the inside with every passing day, as much as I tried to be content and enjoy my natural surroundings. People need other people. It's naïve and pigheaded to pretend otherwise.

And sometimes, people need to double-cross, betray, manipulate, and blackmail other people, too.

CLARITY

It's fun.

As I drive across town to meet my "contact" at the "drop point," I can't keep from grinning. The package I'm carrying might not be explosives or secret codes to detonate said explosives, or microchips with encrypted data that lead to bank accounts containing billions of dollars, but the two little empty plastic vials are rather important to me.

Leslie said I had to wait an hour after eating or drinking to collect my saliva in the vial, so I will have to do it after I meet with my contact. I push my foot down on the gas, speeding only a tiny bit to add some excitement to the trip. Since my car accident, I have been driving like a grandma, so even a little speeding causes my heart to flutter in my chest. I can't wait to deliver "the goods" so that the covert operation to steal my fiancé's saliva can commence. It's just saliva, after all! It's not like I'm stealing his sperm for use with a turkey baster. I giggle a little at the thought. Now that's a covert operation that I would be morally opposed to.

I am hoping that once my associate collects the sample, and I ship the vials off to the doctors at Johns Hopkins, that I will finally be able to breathe and get on with my life. For the past few days I've just been a total mess, and completely unable to write. Sitting at home alone while Liam is at work, and binge-watching Netflix to escape my anxiety just makes me feel like a worthless waste of space.

Any amount of information that I might be able to glean from these DNA tests could be the key to helping me relax and move forward.

I don't want to be one of those women who considers merely being pregnant a replacement for a full-time job. Of course, it's an important job and I'll need to spend a lot of effort on eating right and exercising, and just taking care of myself more in general. I might go to pregnancy yoga classes, or get prenatal massages. I will do all the personal pampering that I never cared to do before, because it won't just be for me anymore.

But that's not all I'll do. No matter what, I will endeavor to be disciplined and keep writing.

Pregnancy is not a free pass to unlimited Netflixing. Not even if it's *really great* Netflixing.

The whole point of having a baby is to create. That is also the whole point of my writing. I simply can't get enough of some of the intense and masterful television shows that have been released in recent years, and the visual pleasure can be overwhelming to a girl who has only *listened* to TV for damn near a quarter of a decade. But while the multitude of magical series is alluring and seductive, I simply start to hate myself when I deteriorate into being solely a *consumer*. I just vegetate until I am a lump of mush on the couch, living only vicariously, and absorbing information and feelings that other people want me to feel. No, I won't allow it anymore. Not without moderation.

I have my own stories to tell, and stories to *live*. My constant, desperate need to escape into the stories of others, the stories created by others; it's a sign that something is deeply wrong. Something is missing. I should be one of those people *writing* those amazing TV shows!

For the first time, I admit to myself that I don't just want to have a baby because of Liam and my family. I have always wanted to have children, for myself. It is a deep and overwhelming desire that I tried to suffocate. For much of my life, I doubted whether I would ever be able to really find love. There weren't too many men who were interested in a blind girl, and their interest was usually temporary. I had completely given up when I locked myself away in New Hampshire; I had given up on love, and life, and family.

Liam woke up all my latent desires. He showed me that I could have all the things I never dreamed would be in the cards for me. How dare he come into my life and give me so much hope and excitement for the future? How dare he propose to me over and over again, and make all these promises of love and success and happiness?

It's all his fault. He's the one who made me believe I could even dare to be happy. Really, truly happy. He's not allowed to get scared and withdraw from me now. He's not allowed to throw this all away. And I think it's completely justified that I'm stealing his DNA.

I'm feeling high on these thoughts, and revved up by the little drive when I pull into the underground parking garage of an elegant new skyscraper. I pull into the visitor's parking area, and park my car next to a familiar Subaru Forrester. I feel like a superspy again when I turn off my vehicle and scan the area for witnesses.

There is a dark, shadowy figure sitting in the driver's seat of the Subaru. He is no doubt waiting for me to drop off the package before he makes his getaway. Stepping out of my car carefully, I walk around my vehicle to the car beside me. I continue looking around to be extra alert of my surroundings, and I keep my hand on my hip, as though I have a secret gun holstered there for protection.

I slide into the driver's seat of the Subaru, and turn to my liaison with an expressionless look on my face.

"He can never know that I'm the one behind the kidnapping," I say softly. "Are you sure you can be discreet?"

The man sitting in the driver's seat holds out his hand in annoyance. "Of course. Do you have the stuff?"

I reach into my purse and pull out the sealed Ziploc bag containing the plastic vial for Liam's sample. "You have to get it back to me tonight, so don't delay. I'm on a deadline here."

"I can work on a deadline," the man says quietly. Then his tone shifts abruptly and he begins to whine. "You're so mean, Helen! I can't believe you're making me do this. It's going to completely ruin his bachelor party! Will you take off those dorky sunglasses? I know you want to look super cool, but we're in an underground parking lot, and it's already dark!"

Stupid Owen. He had to go and ruin my spy fantasies.

Taking off my sunglasses, I sigh. "It doesn't ruin his bachelor party. In fact, it makes it even better because you're kidnapping him when he doesn't expect it. And you're guaranteeing that he will get drunk enough to pass out. I bet the original bachelor party that he agreed to wasn't nearly as wild as this one is going to be!"

"Sure," Owen says grumpily, "but you're making me betray my best buddy. On *the one day* when men are supposed to unite in solidarity against women. This is such an atrocious violation of the bro-code that I should be put in bro-jail."

"Well," I say, leaning forward, "that's why you can't get caught. Bro-jail is a hard place, for hardened felons, and you won't last a day there."

"Ugh. Remind me why I'm doing this?" Owen asks.

"Because you lied to me for months when we met. You never warned me that Liam was being paid to seduce me and only dating me for the sake of his career."

"But it all worked out! And you guys are going to live happily ever after!"

"And if it didn't work out? Liam would have broken my heart, using me as a stepping stone on his way to success. I would have been crushed. You're just lucky that he fell in love with me, too, or you would have been an accessory to *his* crime."

"Lying to a girl and leading her on a little isn't a crime," Owen grumbles.

"Really, Owen? So you had nothing against what he did? Lying to a sweet, innocent girl who was just minding her own business in a pretty little forest…"

"You weren't that sweet and innocent," Owen objects.

"A good girl who had been through so many awful things, that her poor little heart simply couldn't handle one more heartbreak…"

"Dammit, Helen. That's not fair! That's just dirty! You're playing the rape card."

I give him an evil smile, as if to point out that I have him checkmated.

"Fine!" Owen says dramatically, throwing his hands up in the air. "You win! But only because Liam seems really stressed out lately, and I think that getting him so pissed drunk that he loses consciousness is just what he needs tonight. A real bro would only ever hurt his bro if it was also helping his bro."

"You tell yourself whatever you need so that you can sleep at night," I say flippantly as I toss my hair over my shoulder and step out of the vehicle. "Just get the job done."

"Have you been watching a lot of spy movies lately, Helen?" Owen asks me with a raised eyebrow.

"That information is classified," I respond.

"I'm so confused," Owen says.

"Just remember to use the vial before midnight, or it will self-destruct."

"Riiighht," Owen says, nodding enthusiastically and saluting. "I'm on it, boss. Besides, once you see how amazing Liam's DNA is, and how perfectly it will match up with yours to make the most amazing babies on the planet, you'll be begging him to saturate you with his swimmers. And a bro only hurts his bro if it will eventually lead to him getting laid a lot in the future. Vigorously."

"Ewww, Owen!" I shut the door of his car and step away. He winks at me and rolls down the window.

"Hasta la vista, sista," Owen says in a suave way as he peels out of the parking spot and blasts out of the underground.

Okay, that was pretty cool.

Feeling entertained by my spy adventure, and certain that it will lead to satisfactory results, I head over to the elevators. I have another associate to meet with in this building, but she is sophisticated and doesn't do business in the underground parking garage.

No, she's way too classy and white collar for this kind of location. She's a femme fatale, a blonde bombshell, and she even killed a man once when he tried to mess with her.

Besides, if the boys are having an early bachelor party and getting drunk out of their minds with strippers, I might as well spend some quality

time with my sister.
Maybe we'll have tacos and tea.

Chapter Six

Dr. Liam Larson

I feel myself being roughly shaken, and I try to force my eyelids open.

"Good morning, sunshine," says the older female doctor who's standing over me. "Up late last night pleasing the fiancée?"

"No," I mumble, dragging myself off the couch in the break room. "It's insomnia or something."

"Pre-wedding jitters?" she asks, munching on an energy bar. Dr. Jennifer Keating isn't my favorite person in the world, but she's a good doctor.

"Something like that," I tell her, rubbing my eyes.

"So when's the big day?" she asks, fishing into her pocket for a second energy bar to offer me. "And did my invitation get lost in the mail?"

"It's going to be a very small wedding," I explain to her as I take the energy bar with a grateful nod. "It's also all the way in Michigan, so we didn't want to inconvenience people to make the long drive or flight."

"Ooh," Jennifer says, biting off another chunk of her energy bar. "What's in Michigan?"

"My fiancée's family used to own a winery out there, and that's where her parents got married. Their old house was converted to a bed and breakfast, so we booked it for a weekend getaway for the family. We would have invited more people, but the location is pretty isolated and there aren't many other hotels nearby, so it would have gotten complicated."

"Sounds like you rehearsed those excuses," Jennifer says as she polishes off her snack. "But it also sounds like it's going to be a lovely wedding."

"I think so," I tell her with a smile. I actually am looking forward to the event.

"Good job on marrying into money," she says with a wink before turning and heading to the kitchen. "Might have to start calling you Cinderella, Dr. Larson."

"Please don't," I say with a groan. When she is gone and I reach for my phone to check for messages, I realize that my shift was over five minutes ago. Nearly jumping up, I rush to grab my jacket and get out of here. It's a struggle to keep my eyes open as I head for the elevators, and when I file into the small space with a few other people, I find myself asleep on my feet in the time that it takes us to get to the ground floor. I don't think anyone notices, and when the elevator doors slide open with a *ping*, so do my eyes.

Clearing my throat, I move forward with the hustle of other people rushing around in the hospital. I allow my feet to carry me out of the lobby in a daze, and when I step out onto the street, I find myself assaulted by blinding sunlight and squinting in pain. I know that it isn't that bad—I can only imagine how my patients with eye infections feel on a bright, sunny day like this. I should be thankful that the only thing wrong with me is extreme tiredness, and serial napping.

Maybe Helen is right. Maybe I should see a doctor.

I just see so many doctors on a daily basis that I am sick of seeing them. Sighing and tucking my hands in my pockets, I resign myself to walking down the street. I am struggling to keep my eyes open, even while walking, when I feel someone grab my shoulder.

I don't have time to think. The hand feels like it has the intent to do harm. It is strong, aggressive, and clearly meant to drag me toward the street. My body moves before I do, and I am thankful that my reflexes aren't too impaired by my exhaustion. My elbow darts backward first, connecting with my assailant's face. I hear the sound of my bone connecting with his nose, but I continue to grab his arm and twist my body.

Before I have time to realize what I'm doing, I have thrown my attacker to the ground and he is lying flat on his back and staring up at me in shock.

When I see his face, I am immediately filled with guilt.

"What the fuck, man!" I say in exasperation as I stare down at my friend's bloody nose. "Don't you know better than to sneak up on me and grab me from behind?"

Owen lies sprawled on the ground, wincing and clutching at his injured face. "Dude," he says hoarsely. "Will you please just let me kidnap you for your bachelor party?"

Sighing, I stoop down to check out his nose. I reach under his arm to help him stand up, and blood starts dripping down over his lips and chin. He wipes it away with a sniffle.

"I'm really not in the mood for a party right now," I tell him, "but I appreciate the invitation."

"You can't refuse," he tells me, pulling away. "If you won't come with me willingly, I will have to resort to physical force to take you."

A smile causes my lips to crack. "Yeah, because using physical force on me worked out so well for you the last time."

"I don't care! I might not know judo, but I can take you. I'm scrappy and fast," Owen says, getting down into a sloppy boxing stance. "I'm kidnapping you today, Liam, and I'm not taking no for an answer!"

"Fine, fine," I say, holding up my hands in

defeat. I don't want to hurt Owen any more than I already have. "You can kidnap me. But isn't it a little early for the bachelor party? The wedding is still almost two weeks away."

"That's why it's a surprise," Owen says, holding his bleeding nose. "Because I'm the best at surprises! Owww. Did you have to hit me *so* hard, Liam?"

"You snuck up on me from behind, man! You're lucky I'm tired; I could have broken your face."

"It feels like you *did* break my face," Owen says glumly.

"Maybe we should go back into the hospital and get you checked out," I tell him gently. "We can have the party another time."

Owen holds his nose proudly and stands up a little taller with defiance. "I might be in minor need of medical attention, but we'll just have to ignore that, because today is the day that you must be kidnapped! So get ready to get drunk, and take shots, and let loose, and have the party of a lifetime! You're getting married, and *we* are going to Atlantic City!"

Somehow, his excitement is infectious, and I feel myself starting to smile.

"So get in the car," Owen orders, gesturing to his new Subaru Forrester. He pulls out a piece of cloth and holds it up sheepishly. "And maybe you could put on this blindfold and pretend like I actually overpowered you?"

"Sure thing, buddy," I say, grabbing the blindfold. "When we tell the girls this story, we'll say that you're the one who knocked me to the ground. I'll say you had me bound and gagged, and I was so scared for my life, I thought I was actually being kidnapped by the mafia."

"I appreciate that," Owen says as we walk to the car, "but they'll never believe you. You know, this is your fault. If you were a normal guy with more guy friends, then I wouldn't have to subdue you all on my own."

"One good friend is enough for me; especially when that friend is you, Owen. All other guys are just boring and bland in comparison."

"Aw, shucks," Owen says, and it looks like he's getting emotional. "I don't deserve all this sweet talk. You're the bachelor, and I should be making you feel special today."

"I already feel special," I assure him. "No one has ever almost-kidnapped me before."

"The first of many exciting events that will occur on this day!" Owen declares as he moves toward his vehicle.

I don't know what he has planned, but I could use a drink and some laughter right now.

Chapter Seven

Helen Winters

"I mean, I kind of let him abduct me," Carmen says as she sips on her tea. "I knew I needed to get close to him if I was ever going to take him down, legally or otherwise. I really just wanted to put him behind bars, but after what he did to my baby… and to Dad… and what he was trying to do to me…"

"You don't have to talk about it if you're not comfortable," I tell her.

She shakes her head. "It's good to talk about it. I'm slowly getting past it. I've been reading a lot about kidnapping and abduction. I've been trying to face what happened instead of running away."

"But you hardly ever leave this penthouse," I point out. "I barely get to see you."

Carmen smiles. "One step at a time, baby sister. I am just scared of meeting new people. It's no secret that I have poor judgment in general when it comes to people. I used to just see everything through rose-colored glasses, like a blithering idiot.

Loretta Lost

I think I need to spend some quality time by myself and figure out why I've made some of the mistakes I've made before going out into the world again."

"I can understand that," I tell her with a nod as I sip my own tea.

"So, how is the writing coming along?" Carmen asks. "I really loved your last book, and I can't wait to read more."

"I've just been kind of stuck lately," I confess. Things have really changed with Carmen in the past few months. Since she was nearly killed, she has really changed. She has been more attentive, more caring, and more... adult. I always found her overbearing and so positive that it couldn't be real in the past, but now all of that charisma is gone. She's quiet and pensive, and she's not afraid to be honest about the fact that she's sad.

It's funny. I love the way she has grown and matured over such a short period of time, but I do miss the old Carmen. It is clear to see that this Carmen is just a scarred version of the optimistic girl I used to know. There is a certain darkness behind her eyes, like she is always seeing the shadows of the bad experiences she suffered. Losing her husband, losing her baby, and nearly losing Dad—I wish she hadn't had to experience all that.

I thought I was messed up after seeing Grayson hang himself. Messed up enough to drive my car off a cliff and temporarily forget the dreadful sight I had seen.

But I didn't even know what messed up meant. Having to kill a man in cold blood? That will mess you up. Having to look someone in the eyes when you pull the trigger and take their life? Feeling their dead body collapse on you, and knowing you were responsible for snuffing out their entire existence?

It's chilling to think that after all the horrors I've been through, there are still worse situations out there to experience. There are always worse feelings to be felt, and more dangers to be damaged by. It's enough to make anyone want to get holed up in a little penthouse condo, or a cabin in the woods, and have all their food delivered, so they can never go outside again.

People can be terrifying. After a truly traumatic experience, it doesn't just feel safer to hide away from the rest of the world—it feels like the only option. But I suppose that Carmen is hiding away with much more maturity than I did; at least she still accepts visits from family and friends, and allows Owen to spend a lot of time here with her. I guess hiding away doesn't have to feel so lonely, after all.

I wish I had known that. I wish I had known that I didn't have to run away from my family. But maybe we are just very different people, and I needed that.

"I'm sorry," Carmen says softly. "I'm supposed to be doing something fun with you, aren't I? We're supposed to be having an early bachelorette party."

71

"No, no," I tell her with a wave of my hand. "I am cool with just sitting and talking to you. We don't have to do anything crazy."

"Well, at least let's talk about something fun," Carmen says, putting her tea down and narrowing her eyes thoughtfully. After a moment, I see a familiar mischievous expression transform her features. "Are you sure you're ready to forsake all men forever for Dr. Liam Larson? Is he really that special?"

I nod, although our recent problems do make me feel a tiny twinge of doubt. "Yes, he's pretty special," I respond.

"What about that guy you had that little sexual adventure with?"

My eyebrows knit together in confusion. "Are you confusing me with someone else?"

"No, I mean that artist who painted you *in the nude*. Weren't you even a little attracted to him?"

"That wasn't a *sexual adventure,* Carmen!" I say with a little laugh. "Grow up. David is just a friend."

"A friend who stared at your naked body for hours," Carmen says, lifting her eyebrows suggestively. "He's coming to the wedding, right? So I'll get to meet him? Is he hot, or just a weird and artsy hipster?"

"I don't know," I say with a shrug. "He looks normal."

"Normal?" Carmen asks, leaning forward. "What's normal?"

"You know—he has blonde hair like yours, and these really sweet blue eyes. He looks very innocent and almost angelic, like he couldn't hurt a fly."

"Sounds like the opposite of Liam," Carmen muses. "So don't you wonder what you're missing out on? What if tall, dark, and super serious, gloomy doctor isn't your type?"

"What are you even talking about?" I ask her with a little frown. "I love Liam."

"Yes, sure, sure. But you've never really *tried* to love anyone else. From the first time you opened your eyes, there he was, the first man you had ever seen. I can see why you'd get attached and not want to experience anything or anyone else."

"Carmen, I was already falling in love with him before I could ever *see* him. We had already slept together before the eye surgery. It's not like I just fell in love with the first man I ever laid eyes on. The first man I ever laid eyes on just happened to be someone I was already growing to love, who was bending over backwards to help me be able to see."

"You're not confusing gratitude and trust with love and desire, are you?" she asks me. "Because you and Liam went through this whole journey together, of healing you. Do you really think the relationship will continue to last when you don't need his expertise anymore? When he can't get those ego boosts from being your knight in shining armor?"

"Liam doesn't need me to boost his ego," I say in confusion. "He's a doctor, and he helps people every day."

"And what if he ends up falling in love with one of those new patients? Do you really feel secure in the fact that he won't stray when a new damsel in distress with broken eyes comes around for him to save?"

"Yes," I say simply.

"And do you feel secure in the fact that you won't feel tempted by all the sexy, angelic looking blonde men who want you to strip down butt naked so they can stare at your body for hours while they paint you?"

I take a deep breath as I consider the memory. It was a very exciting experience, but I didn't consider it sexual. "Carm, you don't need to drill me with these questions. I thought we just agreed that people are scary and that's why you're not going outside anymore. Surely you can understand that I have no desire to sample all the various men of the world like appetizers at a buffet."

"So is that why you're marrying him?" she asks. "Because you don't want to try anything new? Because you want to feel safe? I guarantee you that kind of thinking will backfire, and someday you will be tempted to try something new, just for the thrill of it."

"I won't," I assure her. "Liam is... he's just everything I could possibly need or want. We're going through a little rough patch right now, but there's still no one I'd rather..."

"Rough patch?" Carmen asks with interest, like a hawk zeroing in on its prey. "You guys are almost newlyweds! You shouldn't be experiencing any rough patches at all. Do you want to talk about it?"

"No, not really."

"Come on! I'm your big sister. You gotta share."

"It's just... Liam is having these nightmares and he isn't sleeping much. Something about his mother, and a baby. We've been trying and failing to conceive for three months, and I think it's getting to him, and he's getting very irritable at even the slightest mention of babies. I don't know what's going on with him, but it might just be a lot of pressure at work, causing him to crack."

"That's interesting," Carmen says gently. "Can I suggest something totally weird and way out there? Liam would probably never go for it, but it's worth a shot."

"Sure," I say with a shrug.

"Since the whole situation with Brad, I've having trouble sleeping and a lot of nightmares too. I started seeing a therapist—but not just any therapist—a hypnotherapist. Yes, I know it sounds crazy, but it's incredibly calming, and it's helped me to make peace with what happened. I would highly recommend my guy to help your guy."

"I'll let him know about it," I say, feeling curious about the hypnotherapy. Carmen never mentioned it to me before. Then I remember that this is Liam we're talking about, and I sigh. "I highly doubt he'll be interested. I mentioned a shrink yesterday and he got upset and stormed out. I also wanted him to do genetic counseling with me, but he refused to give a sample of his DNA. He's really not being cooperative lately."

"Sounds like he's being a stubborn manly man who wants to suffer in silence," Carmen says. "Seriously, I know the hypnotherapy sounds bogus, but it's really been helping me. I swear by it."

"Okay," I tell her with a smile. "Give me the info and I'll look into it."

"Awesome!" she says, reaching for her phone. She looks up at me after a second. "Hellie? I'm sorry I sound like such a bitch, asking all these mean questions. I know that you and Liam love each other, and I really like him and support you two as a couple. I just…"

When she trails off and stares into space, I wait for a while before prodding her. "What is it, Carm?"

"I got married to the wrong man, and it didn't work out for me," she says quietly, with a self-deprecating smile and shrug. "You tried to warn me and I should have listened. And just look at all the crap I've been through because of that bad decision. I just wish I could do the same for you, and be wise and helpful and somehow contribute to your choices, but you've always been so sure of your direction, Helen. You don't really need me."

"Of course, I do," I tell her.

"I wanted to discuss every possible thing that could go wrong before you make this commitment. I don't want you to get blindsided. I want you to be absolutely, one hundred percent sure."

"It would be silly to say I'm one hundred percent sure," I tell her. "There is no guarantee when it comes to love. People are fickle and weak; they get tempted, they get scared, they get desperate, they get lazy. People change. People fail."

"So why bother getting married at all?" she asks me. "If you don't try, you can't fail."

"Because I love him. And I don't want to live any more of my life without being able to call him my husband."

Carmen smiles. "That's a good reason."

Chapter Eight

Dr. Liam Larson

I honestly did not expect Owen's surprise to be so thoughtful. After we arrived in Atlantic City, he did not drive me to a strip club like I expected. Nor did we check into a fancy hotel room to invite strippers for a private stag party, the way many of our college friends did.

No, my best buddy had booked us a manly spa date, complete with deep tissue massages, and relaxing in the sauna while being served all the booze we wanted by attractive female attendants. It was luxurious pampering without the skeezy feeling of most American entertainment. Instead, it felt more the way I would imagine that a Japanese hostess bar would feel.

Frankly, I'm just amazed that Owen is being the responsible one for a change. He has declared himself the designated driver and limited his consumption, while allowing me total freedom to let go. As the alpha male, I am usually the one in charge of taking care of everyone, and I never really get a chance to cut loose. But Owen is quickly coaxing me into relaxing a little, and I am beginning to trust him.

After all, if I can't trust my best friend, who can I trust?

Five drinks later, and I am feeling reeeeaaal good. Owen is really winning me over with this therapeutic, and unexpectedly mature bachelor party. I was really afraid I would have to pretend to be amused by strippers with bare breasts flapping in my face. Now, we are sitting at an elegant restaurant in a hotel resort, having a drink and staring out at the boardwalk.

"Are you sure you can get me back home in time for work tomorrow?" I ask him, and I notice that I am slurring over my words.

"Of course! Don't worry, man. I'm all over it."

"Good," I tell him, lifting my drink and taking a swig. "You're the best."

"Do you think you're drunk enough for blackjack?" Owen asks me with a nudge as he gestures to the casino floor.

Inhaling deeply, I stare in the direction of the tables. I don't know if it's the fact that I have a lot of history in all of these casinos that is making me emotional, or that I am more buzzed than I've been in a long while, but the whole room spins slightly in my vision. "Man, I think I might be *too* drunk for blackjack."

"No way. Liam Larson, the Lion of the Tables is never too drunk for blackjack!" Owen says, with unwavering faith in my skill.

The magnetic pull of the game is strong, and I almost feel like my entire body is swaying toward the casino floor. "I don't think it's a good idea," I tell him slowly, as I glance warily at the tables. Memories of all the various victories and defeats that I suffered while in college come rushing back to me. I promised myself that once I was an adult with a real job, I would never go back to being the crazy gambling kid that I used to be.

"Why not?" Owen asks in disappointment.

"Because I'm going to have a wife in a few days, man. The only reason I used to take such big risks was because I had nothing to lose. But now I do. I can't gamble away every cent I own anymore. It's not acceptable. I actually have some savings—and more responsibilities. Car payments, mortgage, credit cards, student loan payments—all the payments. So many payments. I don't want to be the gambling addict who throws everything away over a game."

"Good," Owen says with a nod. "You passed the test. But I figure we can still grab a drink and walk around to reminisce about the good old days. Maybe you could say a proper goodbye to the tables."

I smile at the concept. "It doesn't hurt to look,

I suppose."

"I'll go order our drinks and pay our tab," Owen says, standing up to head over to the bar.

While he does that, I also get up and slowly stroll in the direction of the tables. I stand at a safe distance, just outside the thick atmosphere of despair. Dozens of men are hunched over their chips and betting mechanically, hoping they can get out of here alive.

I remember it all so well: the euphoric feeling of being *up* and unsure of whether to leave, or to try and win a little more—the sinking feeling as the luck drastically changes, and the winnings all disappear, plus the buy-in. Refusing to take a loss, and buying in for even more—and if my bank account was empty, using credit—having that foolish determination to make back losses and leave with anything above even. I remember my heart beating right out of my chest, the emotions running high, the double downs on big bets, and the splits that seemed to go on forever. I remember pulling piles of chips over to my side of the table, and the dealer making 21 and quickly stealing back all the money on the table, and dashing all our hopes.

I remember staying up for days and days, staring down at the green felt of these tabletops and expecting them to decide my destiny for me. I remember the exhaustion and the misery when nothing would go right, and heading to the cashiers for yet another cash advance off a credit card. I remember the rare occasions when I had a lot of winnings to cash out, and there was a charming gentleman from the IRS waiting to take a chunk away for Uncle Sam.

I remember how I could never really celebrate a win, because the money would go so fast, and it wouldn't be nearly enough to compensate for the previous losses. I remember being so poor that I would have done nearly anything for a few thousand dollars, and putting myself through insane amounts of unnecessary stress. The only reason they called me the Table Lion was because I played with the determination of a man who needed to gamble to make enough money to eat. None of my peers could understand the gravity of my situation.

None of them had a father like mine.

Being around the tables takes me back to a dark place in my life, when I didn't know if I'd be able to finish med school. When I didn't know if I'd be able to pay my rent. When I felt like an outcast among a mostly privileged generation, who barely studied or cared about their school, and just played video games all day.

Even in school, Owen was my only real friend. I remember the days when we'd have to split a bagel between us for lunch, because we couldn't find enough change in the sofa for anything more.

Smiling, I look to the bar where Owen is waiting on our drinks. We have come so far.

The casino was both a blessing and a curse back then, sometimes making things magically better for a short period of time, and sometimes

making things impossibly worse. I remember the days when we had to sleep in the car because we had lost all our money and couldn't afford gas to drive back home, and it was unthinkable for us to afford a cheap motel to crash at. Those days seem so long ago, and it was really thoughtful of Owen to bring me here, so that I could feel deepened gratitude for my new station in life.

There were times when the progress was so slow that it barely seemed like I was moving forward at all. There were times when I had to take such large steps backward that I never thought it was really possible to get past all the boundaries that stood in my way. But being here, and looking at this place, really makes me realize that things have gotten better.

This casino floor is a time portal; it's like gazing at a snapshot of who I used to be. Where I used to be.

But I don't belong here anymore. I have moved past needing this.

Even though I seemed "good" at gambling to most, and I did make some money now and then, I really was just an addict. I was gambling with the thought in my mind that if I had a really great day, I could win a huge chunk of money that could massively change my life, and alleviate all my stress. I thought I could speed things up, and get where I was going faster. If I could turn a hundred bucks, four measly green chips, into a thousand bucks, and turn those ten black chips into ten thousand dollars, then why couldn't I ever turn those ten orange chips into a few hundred thousand dollars and complete financial freedom? I kept thinking that I somehow deserved such a stroke of good fortune. I was somehow better than everyone else, and I deserved having destiny throw me a life preserver when the chips were down.

But if I learned anything from the casino, it's that destiny doesn't owe me jack squat. If I want to create a future, I need to build it with my own two hands. Money earned through ill means doesn't last—it is only the money earned from good, honest work that stays with you in the long run. There are no shortcuts in life, and anything worth having isn't easily or quickly obtained. It takes hard labor; blood, sweat, and tears.

Maybe it's the alcohol, or the massage, but I'm already feeling really uplifted.

Owen has somehow managed to steal away all my pain and fear, and make me realize that I am ready to get married. I'm not the same little boy that my father used to stomp all over, all those years ago. I'm not the same depressed adolescent who didn't know how he was going to make it through the day. I'm not alone anymore. I'm past all of that.

Moving toward the bar where my best friend is ordering our drinks, I feel my spirits soaring. When I clap Owen on the back, he seems startled and he spills one of the drinks slightly, but I am too tipsy to care and I just chuckle.

"Liam!" he says anxiously. "I didn't see you

there behind me. Up for a drink?"

"Sure, buddy. But I don't think I want to gamble tonight."

"That's fine," Owen says, brushing some of the spilled drink off his pants hastily, before handing me the glass. "I don't have the stomach for gambling these days. Watching the way you used to play would damn near give me a heart attack, Table Lion."

"There were some good moments, weren't there? I was pretty wild." A grin settles on my face and I take a large gulp of the drink Owen got for me. There is bit of a funny aftertaste that hits the back of my tongue, but I dismiss it. Owen has been known to order odd drinks, and I might be too drunk to taste things properly.

Owen watches me carefully as I drink, and smiles at me. "You were the champ, Liam. You always were."

"And you were my sssidekick," I say, slurring my words a great deal more than I expected. Clearing my throat, I laugh a little at my own drunkenness and the lack of control I have over my tongue.

"Say, Liam? Can I ask you something?" Owen says quietly.

"Anything, buddy," I say, clapping him on the back affectionately. "You know that we have no sssecrets between us."

"What's going on with you lately? With this bad dream you're having, and telling Helen you're not sure about kids? You really don't seem like yourself lately. What happens in the dream?"

I nod slowly. It takes me a moment to focus on the dream, but once I do, it becomes as clear as day. I begin to feel cold. I begin to feel like I am right there on the road, and I am shivering violently. I am holding the tiny, bloody baby in my arms, and I am afraid. My body physically shakes with the emotions, and I feel myself growing close to tears.

"My... my muddther," I say, and I am vaguely aware that the words are not coming out as I intend them to. I clear my throat and try again. "My modther had a baby in the car. A little girl. My sssister. And it was ssso cold, and there was ssn— snow on the ground."

Owen frowns suddenly, as if in recognition. "I remember you telling me something like this before. You had this dream when we were in college, and you woke up screaming one night."

"Did I? Yesss. It's the worsst nightmare. Because my modther gave me the baby. She wouldn't look at it, or touch it. Thisss tiny infant, covered in blood and plasss—placenta." My tongue feels like it is made of lead as I try to speak, but I don't care as I begin to remember the details of the dream. As the images become clearer, my heart starts to race. Coupled with the amount of alcohol I have had, I start to feel a sense of panic. I place a hand on my chest and take several deep breaths.

"Hey! Liam? You okay, buddy?" Owen asks me with concern, putting an arm around my shoulders.

"N-no. My chest. It hurts."

"Do you want to get out of here, and maybe go sit in the car?"

I am having trouble speaking or breathing, and I can only nod. I allow Owen to guide me out of the bar, and I try my best to remain standing. I don't understand why my limbs feel like jelly and it is so hard to move my body.

Once Owen helps me into the vehicle, I allow my body to sag against the passenger seat. The passenger seat. Just like in my dream. My breathing comes in short, rapid bursts, and I feel like I am having a mild panic attack. If Owen weren't here beside me, I would worry that I was about to die. But I know that he wouldn't let that happen.

"Just calm down, Liam. You're going to be okay," he says, grasping my shoulder tightly. "Can you tell me what happened? In the dream?"

"What if it wasn't a dream."

"What?"

I blink slowly as I try to make eye contact with Owen and communicate my deepest fear. Something about the alcohol is opening the door to the very back of my mind, where the root of the issue has been lingering all this time. "What if I really did that? What if I really killed that baby?"

"Killed?" Owen says in shock, and I can see that his eyes have gone wide. "Liam, what are you talking about? You never told me that the baby was killed."

"I left her there. I just left her there to die. Mama said—Mama said we'd go back for her, but we never did. She said the baby never existed, that it wasss a dream. But what if she did exist? Am I crazy? Am I crazy, Owen?"

My friend just stares at me blankly, and I find myself seized by a sudden anger. I reach out and grab him around the neck, dragging him closer so that I can look into his eyes. "Am I crazy?! Tell me! Did I kill the baby? Was there ever a baby! *Fucking tell me!*"

"Liam," he chokes out, "stop!"

"I can't have a baby. I killed the baby. I'm a murderer. Helen would hate me forever. How can I tell her? That little girl was so tiny. She was like a little kitten. Did she get crushed under the tires of a truck? Did she freeze to death?" I squeeze Owen like a tube of toothpaste to try and get the answers out of him.

He claws at my hands to try to break free. "Hey!" he says hoarsely. "Liam, stop it!"

"Why was I *so stupid?* I killed her, Owen. I know that I killed her. I'm a monster." My hands grow limp, and they fall to my sides. "I'm a *murderer! I'm a fucking murderer!* I knew all along. I was never punished. Not enough. He knows. I know that he knows. He's going to come for me."

My eyelids grow very heavy and it becomes difficult to hold them open. The world is growing dark, and I am beginning to feel like I am underwater. I try to move my arms, but they are flaccid. My whole body begins to feel like it's disconnected from my brain.

I think I hear Owen's voice speaking to me, but it is so far away. I can't make out the words before the world becomes completely quiet and empty.

Chapter Nine

Helen Winters

I have been pacing across the hardwood floor of Liam's studio apartment for what must be hours. It's nearly 4 AM and I haven't heard anything from the boys, even though I've sent multiple texts and voicemails. I'm beginning to worry that their bachelor party got out of hand, and I'm beginning to wonder whether they're coming home at all. Why did I do this? I'm a terrible spy, and I shouldn't have attempted a mission that was so far above my pay grade.

When I hear a key turning in the lock, I rush to the door and help to open it. "Owen!" I exclaim in frustration. "It's so late. Why didn't you respond to my—oh my god!" When I see Owen struggling to drag Liam's lifeless body into the apartment, my heart leaps into my throat and I move to help him. Liam is very heavy, even with his recent weight loss. "What the hell did you do to him?"

"Do you know how difficult it is to get this man drunk?" Owen asks me angrily. "He's a tank!" Reaching in his pocket to retrieve the plastic vial containing Liam's saliva, Owen shoves it toward me. "Here! I hope it was worth it. I had to roofie him."

"You roofied my husband!" I say in outrage.

"Husband-to-be, and yes. There was no other way," Owen says, rubbing his neck and sighing. "Look, Helen. It's been a rough night. I upheld my promise and got you the sample. Let's just get Liam to bed."

Unable to think for a moment, I stare at Owen warily. "Where would you even get the drugs?" I whisper.

"I work in a hospital, remember? Seriously, don't worry, Helen. It's a lot safer to sedate someone with a sedative than to make them pass out from too much alcohol. It's not the first time I've drugged Liam. Here, grab his feet."

My brain starts working, and I take a deep breath. I stoop down to help Owen take Liam to bed, regretting my selfish decisions every step of the way. "Wait," I say suddenly. "You've done it to him before? When?"

"When you were in the hospital, after your car accident," Owen explains as he lifts Liam's upper body onto the bed. "The poor man didn't sleep for a few days, and he was losing his mind. So I slipped something into his coffee."

91

"Oh," I mumble. After we manage to get Liam entirely onto the bed, I sit down abruptly and place my head in my hands. "I never meant to hurt him like this. Am I a horrible person?"

"No way," Owen says, reaching out to squeeze my shoulder. "He's been unreasonable lately, and I understand why you wanted the sample. But I'm not doing anything like this again unless it's a matter of life or death, okay? We're even now."

I nod in agreement, unable to speak. "I'm so sorry, Owen. Thank you. Oh god, what happened to your neck?"

Owen winces and touches some nasty red bruises around his neck, in the shape of handprints. "Let's just say that Liam had a little panic attack. Not related to the medication, but to those nightmares of his. He was ranting... I think we need to get him some help."

"Carmen suggested hypnotherapy," I say softly.

"That might work, but we might need stronger stuff. I don't know if he's delusional, or..."

"Or?" I ask, pushing him for more information. "Owen, spill it. What did you find out?"

He hesitates. "Nothing. I better go. I already betrayed my buddy enough for one night."

"Owen, we're talking about Liam's mental health here. If there's anything you can tell me so that I can try to help him get better..."

"Give me some time to think about it," he says softly. "I need to do some research."

"Okay," I say in a small voice.

Owen notices that I'm really shaken up, and reaches out to give me a hug. "Get those samples tested," he tells me, patting my back. "Make sure you send them off in time, or I drugged my best friend for nothing!" He grins and winks at me before turning to head for the door. "And get some rest, little lady!"

I am finally able to breathe, because Owen's smile makes me feel better. Things can't be that bad if Owen is still smiling, right?

Moving over to the bed, I lean over to place a kiss on Liam's forehead.

"I'm sorry," I tell his sleeping form. "I am so, so sorry for doing this to you. Forgive me."

Feeling the warmth of his skin against my lips, and the steadiness of his breathing, reassures me that he is okay. Of course, he is. Owen would never do anything to hurt his best friend. And he also did this to *help me*. I take several deep breaths, and stand up straighter, clutching the vial of saliva in my hand. Moving back to the kitchen, I open the drawer with the FedEx envelope containing my sample, and add Liam's to the package.

"Mission accomplished," I say weakly to myself, in a lame attempt at humor. "The sample has been successfully acquired."

As I tuck the envelope back into the drawer so that I can mail it first thing in the morning, I am thankful for the fact that I am a writer and not a secret agent. I couldn't stand this much excitement on a regular basis. I would have a nervous breakdown.

Chapter Ten

Dr. Liam Larson

The sound of a door closing causes me to stir. I open my eyes carefully, wondering what city I'm in. Did we end up getting a hotel room after all? Am I going to miss my shift at work today? Or did Owen drive back to New York? I don't remember. This is a little unsettling to me; I haven't been blackout drunk in… ever. Maybe there was one time in high school, but I could have just been really tired. As I pull myself upright, I am expecting my head to start pounding with all the ferocity of a frat-boy hangover, but I am pleasantly surprised that I don't feel too miserable.

I've had worse hangovers after sharing a bottle of wine with Helen.

I am also relieved to see that I am in my own apartment. On the bedside table, I notice a glass of

water and a packet of Alka-Seltzer waiting for me,
with a note:

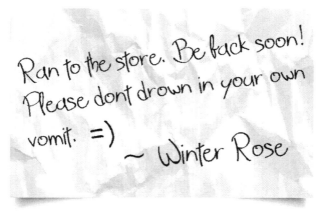

Ran to the store. Be back soon! Please dont drown in your own vomit. =)

~ Winter Rose

Her sense of humor brings a smile to my face.
I am surprised when I hear someone moving around
in the kitchen. Did she already leave and return?
Glancing at the clock, I am surprised to see that it is
nearly 7 AM.

"Helen?" I call out, turning and throwing my
legs off the bed. I am still wearing my clothes from
the night before, and they are wrinkled and
uncomfortable. It looks like someone took off my
shoes, belt, and jacket, but I must have been too
heavy to completely undress.

I hear her footsteps approaching, and I see that
she is fully clothed. "Good morning, sleepyhead,"
she says with a smile. "How are you feeling?"

"Fine, actually," I tell her as I stretch out my

stiff arms. "Kind of well rested. That must have been the most sleep I've gotten in weeks."

"Really?" she asks me in surprise. "Owen only brought you home around 4 AM. You haven't slept that much."

"I haven't been able to sleep for more than an hour without waking up lately—then I have trouble getting back to sleep. Maybe I should get drunk more often. I didn't even have any nightmares." Reaching for the glass of water, I am glad that I don't need the Alka-Seltzer. "So what are you doing up this early? Where did you go?" I ask her.

"I had an errand to run," she explains. "Post office."

"Book-related stuff?" I ask her. "Or wedding related?"

She hesitates. "I guess you could say that it was wedding-related. It's sort of a surprise."

"Mmmm," I say, putting the glass of water down, and moving over to give her a hug. "The only surprises I want are ones that involve your body." I nibble gently on her neck as I tighten my arms around her.

Helen laughs lightly and leans against my chest. "Oh, it definitely involves my body," she tells me mischievously, "And yours. Doing very, very dirty things together."

"Do I get a sneak preview?" I ask her, but my phone starts beeping and I groan as I step away and search for it in my pocket. "Rain check on that. I have to shower and head to work. I don't even remember what happened with Owen last night, so I have no idea how filthy these clothes are."

"But you're feeling okay?" she asks me gently, placing her hand against my forehead and running it over my hair. "You sure you don't want to take the day off work?"

"For a little hangover?" I ask her in surprise.

"I just don't know how exhausted you are after yesterday," Helen says with concern. "You worked all day, and partied all night."

"Helen, I'm not that old," I tell her teasingly. "I can handle a late night and a little alcohol. As long as I don't get drunk like this on a regular basis, you won't need to send me to AA." I am turning and heading for the shower when she clamps her hand around my elbow to keep me from leaving.

"Liam!" she says. "I'm really worried about you. I don't know what happened with you guys last night, but Owen had some pretty bad bruises."

My eyes narrow in confusion. "What?" I ask haltingly. "Did I...?"

"Yeah," she says softly. "He said it was something to do with your nightmares?"

My throat constricts a little. What did I say? What did I do? The dark feeling starts creeping across my chest again. "I'll apologize when I see him today. For now, I'd better shower and head to work."

"No, Liam," Helen says pleadingly. "Something's wrong. And you keep rushing out before we even get a chance to really talk..."

"I'm just busy, love. I wish I could spend more time with you, but if I'm not at the hospital…"

"You can't work twelve hours a day on barely any sleep," she accuses me. "Liam, you're close to full-blown burnout."

"I've always spent long hours at work, Helen. You know this about me. I've experienced burnout before, when I was doing my residency, but this isn't even close."

"But the nightmares…"

"Are not related to me being overworked," I assure her.

"Still, you tried to harm Owen,'" she tells me softly. "I think we should get you some help. We should talk to someone."

"I can't!" I snap at her, and I immediately feel guilty when she flinches. I did not intend to sound so angry. Taking a deep breath, I shake my head. "Don't you understand that if I have any kind of documented mental illness, it could cause me to lose my medical license? If I talk to a doctor about my issues, they'll probably diagnose me with depression or something—trust me, there is always a diagnosis. They might recommend medication or therapy, and while it might make me better temporarily, I'll have to disclose it when it's time for renewal. The medical board might put me under investigation and interview my therapist, and he can choose to tell them that I'm unfit to perform as a doctor. I went to school with a girl who lost her license this way. It could destroy my whole life."

"You can't put your career above your health," Helen implores as she tightens her grip on my arm. "There must be something we can do."

I hesitate. "Okay. Maybe I'll ask someone to prescribe me some sleeping pills, so at least I can get some more rest. Once I'm sleeping more restfully, I think the other issues should be easily resolved. Does that sound reasonable?"

"Yes," she says softly. I only then notice that her eyes are puffy and red, like she has been up all night. "But it's not enough."

"I have a buddy at the hospital who deals with a lot of sleep-related illnesses. Maybe I can ask him for some advice, off the record?"

Helen nods hesitantly. "I guess that will work for now."

"Great," I say, moving forward to give her a kiss on the forehead. "Now, if you'll excuse me, I need to wash all the Vegas glitter off my body before my fiancée suspects what happened last night and leaves me standing at the altar."

When she smiles at my joke, I wink at her and head for the shower. I lock the bathroom door and step into the tiled enclosure, before turning on the cold water. I lean forward and let the freezing water wash over my head as I stare down at the tiles. *It's so cold.*

Did I really hurt Owen yesterday? I wish I could remember. Is there really something wrong with me? Even as I stand here, completely awake, the haunting images from my nightmare rush back to me.

"It's so cold. She doesn't even have clothes yet. Can we go back now?"

"There is no baby. There never was a baby."

Chapter Eleven

Helen Winters

"I'm standing outside the bridal shop," I say loudly into the phone, trying to be heard over the noise of the city traffic and people walking by.

"Hellie, I'm sorry. I don't feel up to it."

"You don't even have to change out of your pajamas!" I assure my sister. "The shop is right downstairs. You can just throw on a jacket and get in the elevator, and walk across the street—you should see me waving. It's less than a block away, I swear!"

"As much as I would love to see you in your dress, or try on my bridesmaid dress, I really don't feel ready to leave home right now. I know the clothes will look amazing—we ordered really great styles from the catalogue and took careful measurements."

I sigh in disappointment. "This sucks, Carm.

102

You're my only bridesmaid. I wish you could be here—I never got to do this stuff with you when you got married."

"It's fine. I was marrying a schizophrenic rapist who would soon be dead anyway."

Lifting my eyebrows, I pause before speaking. "It doesn't sound like you're in the greatest mood. I've never known you to cancel on any situation related to clothing, Ms. Fashion Blogger. I thought you'd be all over this."

"The last time I wore a wedding dress, it got covered in blood and locked away in evidence after I shot a psychopath in the face."

"Okay, I can see how that would put a damper on things." Taking a deep breath, I force a smile; even though my sister cannot see it, I am hoping she can hear it in my voice. "Don't worry about coming out. I'll bring the dresses up to you!"

"I'm so sorry, Hellie."

"It's okay. I was always the one who bailed when you asked me to go shopping when we were younger, so you have a really big pile of coupons you can use to bail on me. I'll see you soon!"

Moving to the entrance of the bridal shop, I grasp the handle and walk inside.

A pretty young shop attendant greets me, and I notice that the letters on her nametag read *Kristen*. The name strikes a chord in my memory, and I feel like there is something important I have forgotten. *Someone* I've forgotten.

"I was told that my dresses would be ready for

pickup today," I inform her. "Helen Winters?"

"Oh, yes! They are in the back. If you'll just wait here, I'll prepare a fitting room for you. Are you expecting any of your bridesmaids to join you?"

"No, they're busy today," I lie.

She nods and disappears, and I keep mulling over where on earth I've heard that name before. Did I use it in one of my books for a secondary character? Did I ever know someone named Kristen? Or Kirsten? I try to dig through my brain, and I feel like it's almost there, at the tip of my tongue. Kristina? When I recovered memories from the last three years, it was never complete. It wasn't like the movies where an amnesia patient would suddenly remember everything in a cool montage with music playing.

I had brain damage. I'm lucky that I didn't lose more memories, or even motor skills. There are still gaps missing here and there, and I still regularly learn of events that completely escaped me. Oftentimes, I never would have regained my memory if something didn't remind me of what I'd forgotten—and if I didn't have people in my life to confirm that I was correct about what I remembered.

I pull out my phone and send Liam a text message:

> Picking up my dress now! Quick question: Did I ever know anyone named Kristen?

Delivered

The phone informs me that he is already responding, so he must be on a break at work. But before I can receive his message, the saleswoman returns with a bright smile on her face. "The dress is gorgeous!" she says with excitement. "If you come with me to the back, you can try it on and we can make sure everything is okay."

"Great," I say, following her deeper into the store. When my phone pings, I quickly check Liam's message.

> You had a waitress friend named Krista. Is that who you mean?

Krista. That makes sense. It feels right. And she's a waitress? We were friends? I must have her number in my phone. Maybe I could call or text her. I am trying to imagine her face when the woman I am following stops and turns back to me.

"We only have one bridesmaid dress here. Is that a mistake?"

"No, that's correct," I tell her.

"Must be a small wedding," she comments. "Sometimes those are the best kind! I was supposed to keep it a secret, but your father is here. He said that he wanted to be the first one to see you try on the dress."

"Aww," I respond at once, a soft smile touching my lips. "That's so sweet of him."

"Just right through here," she says, guiding me.

My spirits are lifted to know that someone from my family will be here for this moment. There is something very sad about going to pick up your wedding dress alone. This is the sort of thing that Mom would have loved; she would have been all emotional and taken hundreds of photos. I was never really the type of girl who dreamed about having an elaborate wedding, but I did expect there would be some sweet moments spent with my family.

When I walk through the doorway, I find that my feet are suddenly frozen in place. I try to speak, or move, but my whole body feels paralyzed in shock.

The man who is waiting in the room for me is not my father.

My heart jumps into my throat, and I can hear it beating loudly in my ears.

"Pretty little Helen," the man says in a sickly sweet voice as he uses a cane to stand up. "I've been waitin' for you."

"I'll give you two some privacy," the saleswoman says, turning to leave. "The wedding dress is in room three."

I want to stop her from leaving, but I am too slow.

"You'll be a damn fine lookin' bride," the man says as he limps forward, his arm shaking as he uses his cane. "Is it a pricey dress? It must be. This is a snotty store, and you seem like an expensive little whore."

His foul language snaps me back to reality, and I am able to step away from him, circling toward the windows and out of his reach. "How did you find me?"

"I can tell you come from money. I called a bunch of fancy bridal shops, asking when Helen's dress would be ready. Shoulda figured it would be in a stuck-up part of town, for a stuck-up girl."

"You don't know anything about me."

"I know that you's a snobby rich bitch. Liam wouldn't marry any other kind of whore. The boy doesn't care about pussy. He cares about cash."

"He cares about *me*," I inform Liam's father, stepping away carefully as he advances on me. "And I care about him."

"Bullshit. Think I don't know my boy? He ain't ever cared about no one but himself."

Ignoring this, I study the man's cane. "You

don't need the wheelchair to move around?"

"Looks like my leg's healing up a bit. Seems like I'm not as crippled as I thought."

"That's a pity," I say under my breath.

"Oh, you got a mouth on you! If my woman spoke to me like that, I'd knock her teeth out."

"Probably why she doesn't talk much," I mumble, stepping away from him. How did this man even get into a nice shop like this?

"The only good woman is the kind who keeps her mouth shut," Liam's father sneers at me. "Hope my boy will teach you that before long. Yeah, he'll put you in your place."

"Liam would never hurt me," I say quietly.

"You know him for how long? Few years? I know him his whole damn life. Kid's got a mean streak. Kid snaps and lets loose, then one day you'll find yourself wakin' up in the hospital with a bloody lip, a black eye, and a couple broken bones."

"I know that Liam can fight. I've seen him break both of a man's arms. He taught me how to fight, too, so I could defend myself. He would never hurt someone who didn't deserve it."

"What happens when he decides that you deserve it?" Liam's father asks with a twisted, ugly smile. "The boy is a violent sonuvabitch."

The memory of the bruises on Owen's neck comes back to me. I know I shouldn't allow any doubt to cloud my mind, but I can't help thinking about the DNA test. I *stole* Liam's saliva for a sample to analyze. If he ever finds out, would he be seriously angry?

"You don't have to heed my words," Liam's father says. "But I've come to warn you: don't marry the little prick unless you're prepared to deal with his true colors. There's a cruel beast lurking just under the surface of that pretty little doctor. Like in that story about Dr. Jekyll and the other one."

"I will take your warning under advisement," I respond evenly.

"Also," the man says, swinging his cane at me angrily, "you tell that boy that he better not fucking come near my wife again. If he does, I'll cut off his balls."

"Why?" I ask with a frown. "She's his mother."

"Dunno what he said to her, but the woman's been crying nonstop since they last met. I tried hitting her in the face and telling her to shut the fuck up, but it doesn't work."

I am horrified that he can say this so casually. "You're a monster. I should call the police on you."

"Try it," he challenges me, shaking the cane at my face. "If I go to jail, the woman will probably be dead in a few weeks anyway. She's so weak she can't change her own fucking underwear. Poor woman don't need her son coming around saying no shit to her!"

I shudder as the man's rotting alcohol breath hits my face. Stepping back to avoid his cane, I glare at him. "Well, she can see better now that her cataracts have been removed, so she's probably just crying because of your ugly face."

Liam's father laughs, and it is a bitter sound. "You got some balls on you, eh, girl? You think this is a joke, that the boy is giving my wife grief?"

It seems so absurd that this man beats Liam's mother into complete fear and subjugation, but also seems to care about her, or want to protect her at the same time. "She could be in pain from the surgery?" I suggest. "Although Liam used special lasers to make the cuts, which should minimize pain after the procedure."

"Real fucking fancy, those lasers. No, it's something he said to her. She ain't touched her painkillers. I've been using them to help me get around on this bum leg."

I frown at this. "Her eyes were cut open. Don't you think that she needs the pills more than you?"

"Nah, she ain't need nothin'. Boy did a good job of it; her eyes are fine."

I blink in surprise. Did he just pay Liam a compliment?

"But whatever he said left her real shaken up. She's an old woman, and she can't take his bitchin' and moanin'. That boy never did learn to show his momma no respect."

For a moment, I think I see a side of Liam's father that I didn't expect. He genuinely seems to care about his wife, even though he has a piss-poor way of showing it. What could be bothering Liam's mother? Is it the fact that we didn't invite her to our wedding? I study Mr. Larson's face, and find only sincerity there, until he snarls at me.

"D'you hear me, girl? Tell that little piece of shit that he ain't gonna come near his momma again unless he wants his jewels shot off. I'm not joking. We've been getting along just fine without that ungrateful bastard all these years. Last thing we need is need some pompous, bigshot doctor, saying mean shit and making an old woman cry."

I stare in surprise as Liam's father turns and walks out of the shop, struggling to move at all with his cane. Feeling a bit of pity for him, I have the urge to invite him and his wife to our wedding, or do anything at all to try and mend his relationship with Liam. But it's not my place, and I don't want to meddle any more than I already have. If I keep going against Liam's wishes, he won't be able to trust me at all, and that's not a great way to start a marriage.

When the saleswoman returns, she smiles at me. "Where did your father go? I hope I didn't miss seeing you in the dress!"

"He was my father-in-law-to-be," I explain softly. "I don't really feel like trying on the dress anymore. I'll just pay the outstanding balance for both dresses and take them off your hands."

"But if there are any alterations…"

"I'm sure it will be fine," I tell her. "I don't care about making sure every little detail of the wedding is perfect. I just want to get married to the man I love. Why does it have to be so difficult?"

Chapter Twelve

Dr. Liam Larson

"I'm not sure I'm the person you should be speaking to," Dr. Victor Singh says as we walk through the hospital's neurology clinic.

"Come on, man," I say in a friendly tone. "Just humor me."

"Liam," Victor says with his slight Indian accent, "it sounds like you need the psych ward."

This puts a frown on my face, and I stop walking abruptly. "Do you mean that?"

"No!" Victor says with a laugh. "Just joking, man. Hey, I heard from Harold in pediatrics that his buddy saw you at a casino the other day. Is that true? You went gambling and didn't invite me?"

Wow. If anyone thinks rumors spread fast in high school, they haven't worked in a hospital. "I'll invite you next time, Vick, and we can tear up the roulette table. Just do me a favor and give me your professional opinion? Any advice at all could be a real help."

"The sleeping pills I prescribed you should do the trick," Victor says, tapping the folded paper I have tucked in my pocket. "When you're sleep-deprived, the brain can do all sorts of wacky things. Just keep reminding yourself of one very important fact: *It's not real.*"

"It's not real?" I repeat hesitantly.

"Yes. There are many theories about dreams, but I believe they are just random neural impulses; just your brain having fun at your expense. I mean, you said there's a baby in the nightmare, right? Dreams can be anxiety-related, so chances are you're just freaking out about starting a family since your wife seems to be pressuring you to get her pregnant."

"She's not pressuring me," I object.

Victor laughs. "Women are always putting pressure on men like that. You're probably just experiencing a kind of performance anxiety or feelings of insecurity. Scared you might be impotent?"

"I am not insecure or impotent!" I say defensively, and a little too loudly.

Two female nurses happen to be walking by at this moment, and when they burst into giggles, I feel my cheeks turning red. Meanwhile, Victor is chuckling madly.

"Just relax, Liam," he says with a friendly pat on the back. "Once you get the girl pregnant, your anxiety and nightmares should go away. Until then, just keep reminding yourself that it isn't real. Say it like a mantra. *This is not real. This is not real.* It will remove any power the dreams have over you."

"Thanks, Vick. I'll give it a shot."

"Also, don't be too worried about having kids," Victor adds. "I have four, and the wife is pregnant again. I don't know why you Americans are so afraid of something so natural. Kids make our dull lives colorful and bright—they give you a reason to wake up in the morning and be a better man."

Nodding and smiling, I already feel a little healthier.

"If the pills don't help, I can keep you overnight for observation in the sleep lab. And if that fails, we can lock you away in the psych ward," he says with a wink. "You'll love it there."

"Don't joke like that," I tell him with a shudder. As I turn away and head back to my section of the hospital, I feel my phone vibrate in my pocket. Lifting it out, my heart skips a beat at the message from Helen.

> Your father was waiting for me at the dress shop. He's a messed up guy.

Taking several deep breaths, I respond at once:

> Are you okay?

Yes. Just a little shaken up.

> I just finished my break at work and can't get away right now. Can you come to the hospital? I don't want you to be alone.

Delivered

Sure. Be there soon. 😔

My mind begins spinning with all the reasons that my father could have been waiting for Helen. I want nothing more than to get this prescription filled and go home and take the sleeping pills, but I can't get out of this shift. I booked time off work for my honeymoon in a few weeks, and I'm trying to maintain a perfect record until then. I have

116

already had way too many emergencies that caused me to be absent in the past year.

Chapter Thirteen

Helen Winters

As I pull into the hospital parking lot, I am grateful that Liam asked to see me. I didn't want to be alone. I feel a little pathetic after taking a cab home to Liam's apartment from the dress shop, even though it was so close. I also skipped going to my sister's place, because I didn't want to let her see me while I was all wound up and feeling threatened.

Driving through the hospital parking lot gives me a strange feeling of déjà vu. Once I park and exit the vehicle, I let my feet carry me through the hospital. When I am directly beside the gift shop and café, I turn and look toward the area in puzzlement.

Walking forward curiously, I seem to recall sitting at these tables and talking to someone. I seem to recall being happy. I can't quite put my finger on it…

The scent of good coffee assails my nostrils, along with pleasant female laughter. I see the back of a girl wearing the uniform of a waitress and holding a coffee pot. Her sandy blonde hair is styled in two braids, and she looks friendly and sweet.

Liam's text message comes back into my mind: *You had a waitress friend named Krista. Is that who you mean?*

When the girl turns around, her face displays recognition. "Winter?" the girl exclaims, placing down her coffee pot and moving forward to give me a hug. "Oh my god! I thought I'd never see you again."

"Krista," I say slowly, returning the hug with confusion.

"Where have you been? Why haven't you visited me? How's Liam doing?!" she asks, rattling off questions like an automatic rifle.

"I—I don't remember you," I say in embarrassment. "A few months ago, I crashed my car into a tree. I lost three years of memories, and I haven't regained them all yet."

"Seriously?" she says in surprise. "Oh! And I thought you just didn't like me anymore."

"I'm getting married in less than two weeks," I tell her with a slight smile.

Her eyes widen in surprise. "My goodness, you got engaged! I've missed all these exciting events in your life. This makes me so sad."

When her eyes begin to shine with tears, I feel

guilty and upset that my memories erased this girl from my life. "The wedding is at a vineyard in Michigan, on the fourteenth—would you like to come? I only have one bridesmaid. I mean, I'm sorry if this seems totally out of the blue. I don't remember if we were close enough for me to ask you to be a bridesmaid, but I don't have any female friends other than my sister. This is a huge surprise to me, and I assume we were close."

"Stop rambling!" she says, wiping her eyes. "I would love to be your bridesmaid, Winter. We were good friends. But... but I have exams that week. I can't make the trip that weekend. If it were only the weekend after! You know how tight my schedule is, between school and waitressing—actually, silly me, you probably don't know."

"I am starting to remember more about you," I tell her with a smile, "the more I listen to you speak. Everyone calls me Helen, now, by the way."

"You'll always be Winter to me."

We share a smile, and suddenly, it does feel like we are old friends.

"I have to get back to work," she says suddenly when a group of people walk into the café. "Do you have time to sit and wait for me so we can catch up?"

"Not right now," I tell her. "I need to go and see Liam. But we'll catch up soon!"

"You better come back, Winter! I'll be super pissed if you disappear again for months."

"I won't forget you this time. I'll be back

soon," I promise, before turning and heading out into the lobby.

"Sorry I can't come to your wedding!" Krista calls after me.

I nod and send her a sad smile before heading to the hospital elevators. However, I find myself crashing into a large, hard object. The familiar smell reaches me before I recognize the grip of his hands on my arms.

"Helen," he says softly. "Thank god, you're okay. My father didn't do anything to you?"

"No," I say, wrapping my arms around him tightly. "He was walking around, though. He was waving his cane at me and cursing and threatening—it was a little scary."

"I have about five minutes before I need to go back to work. Can we go sit in your car or something?" he asks.

Nodding, I turn and lead him back to the parking garage. We move toward my car, and I reach into my pocket to unlock the vehicle. Liam opens the door to the back seat, and moves inside, and I move to enter from the other side. Sighing, I lean against him and bury my face in his white lab coat.

Liam holds me close and runs his hand over my hair. "What did my father say?" he asks softly.

"He said that he would hurt you if you went near your mother again. Apparently, you said something that really upset her and she's been crying a lot." I pause and tighten my grip on his body before I continue to speak. "He said that she wouldn't even stop crying when he hit her in the face and told her to stop."

"Jesus," Liam says, inhaling sharply and reaching up to run his fingers through his hair. "I knew that I shouldn't have asked her about that dream. It's just despicable, and basically accusing her of something like that—I probably broke her heart. She's an old woman, and I should have been more considerate."

"I don't know about your dream, Liam," I tell him gently. "But I think that she could be really bothered that she didn't receive a wedding invitation. Why else would your dad stalk me at the dress shop?"

Liam runs his hand up and down my arm lazily. "I guess you're right. Do you really think that I should invite my parents? Maybe just my mother?"

"Just your mother, I think," I say softly. "There's something about your father—I do think he cares, in some deep and twisted way. But he does scare me, and he—he reminds me a little of..."

"Grayson," Liam finishes for me with a nod. "I know."

"Yes," I say, linking my hand with his and squeezing gently for comfort.

Liam kisses the top of my head. "See? This is why I've always understood you, Helen. We have similar demons in our histories, casting shadows over our lives."

"I'm free now," I tell him, lifting my face to place a kiss on his lips. "You will be too, soon."

"God, I hope so." He kisses me back deeply, and then groans and pulls away. "I'm so comfortable here. I wish I didn't have to go back to work."

"Is that the key to your insomnia, Liam?" I ask him teasingly. "Do you just need to sleep in a car to get quality rest with no nightmares?"

He chuckles softly. "I have slept in a lot of cars. I'm also pretty comfortable doing other things in cars, but I don't have the time to show you right now."

"Darn," I say in disappointment.

"On a serious note, I am going to fix my problems, Helen. I have been so irritable and such a jackass lately. I got a prescription for some sleeping pills," he assures me, "and some advice from a great neurologist—someone I trust."

"Neurology? Aren't dreams more in the realm of psychology?" I ask him.

"Only a psych major would say that," he jokes, "but I guess it's a little of both."

We sit in silence for a moment, until Liam squeezes my arm and pulls away. "Okay," he says with a deep breath. "I'll invite my mother to the wedding. As long as my father isn't there, no harm can be done."

"Maybe don't tell her the location so he can't find out and show up," I suggest. "We could just tell her the date, and pick her up."

"That sounds good," Liam says, placing a quick kiss on my lips before opening the car door and stepping out. "I love you," he says softly, before shutting the door.

Sighing, I collapse on the backseat. There is something about dangerous and stressful situations that reassures me that Liam will be a rock solid husband. When life gets hard, he is always able to act fast, be a hero, and stay strong. I think that lately, because life has been a little easier, he has had too much time to think and stress himself out. Liam has had so much stress in his life that he struggles to operate without it, and needs to create it artificially.

It is so cozy here in the car, and I am almost tempted to curl up and take a nap until Liam finishes work. But the price of hospital parking is *crazy* and I need to try to get home before rush hour.

Who am I kidding? It's always rush hour in New York City.

Chapter Fourteen

Three days before the wedding...

Liam lets out a low whistle as he drives up to the gorgeous house overlooking a small lake. "You really grew up here?" he asks in disbelief.

"I guess so," I say in wonder. "At least part of the time. I remember running around and playing in the vineyards, but I didn't have any clue how picturesque it was."

"I thought your house in New York was impressive," Liam tells me, "but this one puts it to shame. This house is basically... a castle."

"You're exaggerating," I say, leaning forward to peer through the windshield. He's really not. The stonework on the exterior of the house does remind me of a castle. My mother used to tell me that she thought this vineyard was the most romantic place on earth. I smile sadly. "Besides, we don't own it

125

anymore, remember? My parents sold it years ago to help with renovations to the house in New York."

We both grow quiet then, thinking the same thought: *the house that is now destroyed.*

"Can you remind me what our schedule is like?" Liam asks as he parks the car and turns to me.

"Sure," I say, looking at the list on my phone. "We have to go to the city hall to pick up our marriage license from the county clerk, meet with the caterers to try the sample dishes, and the cake shop. We have to pick up your tux, and meet with the photographer and videographer and discuss the pre-wedding photo shoot on Friday. Owen will be arriving with your mother on Friday before the rehearsal dinner, along with most of our guests. I need to get a manicure and pedicure and other spa prep with Carmen tomorrow. I need to call and confirm the makeup artist, the florist, the officiant…"

"Whoa," Liam says. "I thought that by having a small wedding we'd escape all this red tape."

"It's not red tape. These are all the details that will make our wedding possible. Maybe even a little special."

"Special! I think you're aiming for magical. Did you really need to spend five thousand dollars on engraved champagne glasses?" Liam asks with a grin.

"They're keepsakes for our guests," I say defensively. "Besides, my last book has been selling fairly well and the publisher gave me a nice advance for the next one. Hey, we *both* loved those champagne flutes, Liam!"

"We did," he admits. "They just seemed insanely expensive to me. Maybe one set of toasting glasses was okay, but you wanted to get them for everyone!"

"Because it's such a small wedding. If there were a hundred people, we obviously couldn't afford to go all out and get everyone the best stuff."

Liam shakes his head. "There are so many things we have to keep track of and pay for—it really adds up. I know that we've been planning for ages, but now that we're here, I feel like we are just hemorrhaging money. And all the appointments are kind of overwhelming—it feels like more work than I have at the hospital."

"Still want to marry me?" I ask him teasingly.

"Heck, yes," he says with conviction, turning toward me with a bright smile.

I am so glad that he has been taking the sleeping pills every night. He seems to have recovered from his nightmares, and he has been more energetic and cheerful this past week. He has also been eating better and hitting the gym more regularly.

When my phone dings with a message, I glance at it and see that it is an email from Dr. C. Nguyen and the subject heading says: *Your DNA results are delayed.*

We are currently processing your information

through a quality review in our lab...

My stomach sinks in disappointment. I have been waiting impatiently for this email and checking my inbox obsessively dozens of times each day.

"Anything important?" Liam asks.

"No," I say nervously, trying to act normal. "Just my publisher asking for an update. I'm going to have to sneak in as much writing as possible while we drive around and do chores before the wedding. Is that okay?"

"For now, Mrs. Larson," he says playfully, sliding his hand over my thigh. "But I hope you're not expecting to get any work done on our honeymoon. I plan to keep you tied to the bed the whole time we're in Paris, and I won't let you leave the hotel room no matter how much you beg for freedom."

"I don't think I'll complain," I say with a smile. "But what about all the cool things we planned to do and see on our trip?"

"They all cost so much money. I think it will be a lot more fiscally responsible if I just pound you until you feel paralyzed from the waist down."

"Liam!" I say in surprise, but my stomach clenches with desire.

"What?" he says innocently. "These are the small details that make our wedding special."

"Or magical," I say with a smile.

Chapter Fifteen

One day before the wedding...

"What do you think of the sleeves now?" Liam asks me as his tux gets fitted.

I nod as I look up to see the tailor pinning the sleeves. "It looks good to me! I don't know much about fashion." Turning my eyes back to my laptop, I try to squeeze out a few more words of my chapter. It has been quite comfy to sit here in the shop and work while Liam gets his clothes sorted out. When my phone pings with the sound of an email, I glance at it expecting it to be junk.

My heart skips a beat when I see the words. *From Dr. C. Nguyen. Your DNA reports are ready*.

Glancing up at Liam furtively, I tilt my laptop screen away from him so he won't be able to see what I'm looking at. Using my phone to create a hotspot, I open my email on the computer and skim over the instructions. Without hesitation, I click the link in the email that leads to our DNA results.

My heart begins to race as I wait for the page to load. My skin feels very cold and goose flesh causes all the hairs on my arms and neck to stand up.

When the page loads, it looks like a normal website. I have to enter my birthdate and my mother's maiden name to gain access, information I had provided in the package. Once I am in, I hold my breath. There are questions that I need to answer before I can even see the information! Do I consent to viewing health information? Yes. Do I consent to viewing ancestry information? Yes. Do I consent to—yes, yes, yes! I click furiously until I get to the end.

Finally. There are a few categories on the screen, and my eyes rapidly scan the information. The medical jargon blurs together in my brain— dozens of diseases float across the screen in two columns, one for me, and one for Liam. I don't know where to look first. There is a category about genetic risks, and it looks like I have a high risk of developing Celiac disease, which surprises me. I've never experienced any issues with digestion, or sensitivity to gluten. I remind myself that the information indicates that there is just a risk, and nothing is for certain.

I exhale. Some of the information is locked, and I need to click on a little padlock symbol and agree that I would like to see it. The first one is for ovarian and breast cancer. I hold my breath until the information pops up on the screen, and it takes me a moment to read that my risk is typical, and not heightened. That's a load off my shoulders—but I quickly click away to read more.

The next bit of locked information is for Alzheimer's disease. I click on the link and give permission to unlock it once again, and my heart sinks to see that Liam has a high risk of developing Alzheimer's Disease. *It's just a risk,* I tell myself. *Knowing this now will allow us to take precautions, perhaps.* I am relieved to see that my own risk for Alzheimer's isn't heightened. *Although it could explain his mother's poor cognitive function...*

After a moment, I realize that I am looking at the wrong category. My eyes were pulled to the column with the risk factors, but what's really important is the section about inherited conditions. It's in alphabetical order, listing a bevy of dangerous conditions from A to Z, or from Autosomal Recessive Polycystic Kidney Disease to Zellweger Syndrome Spectrum—and ultimately, it seems that neither of us are carriers.

Variant absent. Variant absent. Variant absent.

I close my eyes, and exhale. It's okay. I have barely looked at the information, but I know that it's okay. There is nothing glaring that jumps out at me. There are no red flags or sirens telling me that I can't have children with Liam. Our DNA is mostly fine. It's flawed, of course, and we both have the potential for various illnesses, but I know that we'll get through them—or even avoid them by trying to live a healthier lifestyle.

I am sure that the data on this website is incomplete. My LCA isn't even on here. There must be a frightening number of genetic problems that aren't identifiable in our DNA yet. There could be new illnesses to arise, or infections and accidents that have nothing to do with our biology. There could be war or famine, or global warming in our lifetime, but somehow, none of that seems to matter anymore. Everything is going to be okay.

We will probably have a healthy baby.

I feel like I am instantly twenty pounds lighter. This is great, because I do want to look good in my wedding dress. I somehow feel like I could fly, or walk on air.

"Helen? Helen, are you listening to me?" Liam asks curiously. "What are you doing? You've been totally glued to the screen."

"I'm sorry," I tell him quickly. "What were you asking?"

"The hem of the pants. Does it seem like a good length?"

"Sure," I tell him with a nod, not really knowing or caring. "It looks good, Liam. You look great."

"Thanks," he says with a smile, turning back to the mirror.

He *is* handsome, and I sigh a little in contentment. I wish I could rush over and jump on him in excitement to tell him all the good news about our DNA, but he can never find out about how I lied and tricked him. When I look back down at the computer screen, I scan over the information for several minutes until I notice a blinking blue button on the website. *Relative match.* My head tilts to the side curiously, and I can't resist clicking.

Close family: 1
Second and third cousins: 3
Fourth cousins: 15
Distant cousins: 86

My curiosity grows, and I click the "close family" button to see if Dad or Carmen, or one of Liam's parents, might have done a DNA test at some point without my knowledge.

"Oh my god," I whisper, as a cold sweat instantly covers my shoulders. The words flash across my brain. *Find your relatives... other DNA matches... registered in our system... Female... Age 25... California.* I can't believe what I'm seeing. Dozens of snippets of information click into place quite suddenly. One word stands out on the page, with startling clarity.

Sibling match.

"Helen!" Liam says with a little frustration, reaching out to shut my laptop so he can get my attention. "Are you ready to get going?"

I look up in surprise. When did he take off the tux and get dressed in his jeans? Are the alterations already complete? Have I been really been so oblivious, and staring at this information for so long?

"We have to meet with the photographer before the family starts arriving!" Liam tells me, grabbing my laptop and offering his hand to help pull me out of my chair. "Come on, up, up! We have a rehearsal dinner to prepare for."

"I'm sorry," I tell him quietly. "I was just…"

"Engrossed in book research? Helen! That's fine, but you can surely give it a break for a few hours so that we can *get married*. It's kind of important!"

"You're right," I say, carefully taking the laptop back from him. "I should take a break and just focus on us."

"We're only going to get married once," Liam says, sliding his arm around my waist and kissing my shoulder. "Might as well enjoy it."

Chapter Sixteen

When Owen arrives, I stand by the house and wait impatiently as he hugs Liam and two men share some words. It looks like Liam's mother did not make it to the wedding. I wonder why? As Owen moves closer to the house, I fix him with a grave look, and cross my arms over my chest.

"Hey, little lady," Owen says as he approaches me and gives me a hug. "You doin' okay?"

"I need to talk to you," I tell him in a whisper. "Now."

He pulls away slightly and looks at my face to gauge how serious I am. "Is it about... the thing?" he asks.

"Yes," I tell him. "Come on."

He nods and begins following me obediently.

Liam calls after us. "What are you two planning? Owen, if this is Magic Mike-related, I'm not going to be happy! No one wants to see what you have under your shirt."

Turning back, Owen flashes a grin at his

friend, but continues to follow me. I start moving faster into the house, startled by the memory of my feet. Looking at the stairs and doors actually trips me up a little, so I do something that most people would consider a little bizarre.

I close my eyes.

Suddenly, the strange house is familiar again. With my eyes open, this is a house I have never seen before. With my eyes closed, this is a house I have been in many times. This is the house where I spent all the lazy summers of my childhood, and it feels like no time has passed. Even though it is not summer, I can smell the scent of the thousands of grape vines growing around us, and I know exactly where to step.

My hand reaches for the door leading to the basement effortlessly, and turns in the right direction. I am elated as my feet carry me below the house and down to the wine cellar, where I know we will have some privacy. I open my eyes and turn around to look at Owen, who has barely kept up with me. He stares around in surprise at the gorgeous wine cellar, and I am also distracted for a moment.

Everything is familiar, and the nostalgia is overwhelming. But I have business to attend to.

"Where's Liam's mother?" I ask. "Weren't you supposed to drive her here?"

"She wasn't feeling well," Owen explains sadly. "Her husband wouldn't let her leave. I tried, but he nearly gave me a black eye."

"Okay," I say with a nod. "It doesn't matter. Did you do your research? On Liam's dream?"

"I gave it a shot," he says softly, "but I didn't find anything."

"What exactly happened in the dream?" I demand.

Owen hesitates. "Liam was ranting and drunk when he told me about it, but from what I understand… he killed a baby."

"Details, please."

"I don't really know, Helen. It sounds like he was pretty young when it happened, but his mother had a baby girl… and I think she made him leave it at the side of the road to die. Probably some kind of postpartum depression thing. It was cold, and he's not sure what happened to the child. I did some research, but I couldn't find anything. I also didn't have a precise year or a location to go from, and I didn't want to ask him about it again and set him off."

"I found her," I tell Owen. "I found his sister."

"What?"

"The DNA tests we did. They had this feature where they could search for relatives who were in the database. I figure if she was abandoned, or rescued, she must have done the DNA tests searching for her relatives."

"Helen," Owen says with wide eyes. "If we hadn't done that test, we never would have found her."

I nod, feeling tears prick the back of my eyes.

"I didn't contact her yet. I don't know what to do. I want to invite her to the wedding, and buy her a ticket. She's around my age."

"That means he would have been around four when she was born," Owen muses. "We still don't know anything about her. She could be really messed up. If she grew up as an orphan, we don't know if she was adopted or left in foster care. We don't know if she'll hate Liam for what he did and blame him for everything. We don't know..."

"She's Liam's sister," I tell Owen. "That's all we need to know. Isn't this what's been eating him up all this time? He doesn't know what happened to her. He thinks he killed her! Don't you think it would make him happy to know she survived—to meet her and see what she's like?"

"I don't know," Owen says. "Helen, I don't know if you should do this right now. Why don't we wait until after the wedding and sit down and talk to him?"

"Because then she'll miss coming to her brother's wedding," I say softly. "You couldn't get his mother to come, so Liam has no other family here."

"He has me," Owen says stubbornly, "and James."

"Blood relatives," I tell him. "That's important, too. I have my dad and my sister here, and that means the world to me. Even if Liam and his sister have never met each other—they are family. They are connected, and they both deserve to have each other in their lives. To be reunited."

"Helen... you're crazy," Owen says hoarsely. "This could either go really well, or be a complete disaster."

"I'm willing to risk it."

"Do you... do you even know her name?" Owen asks.

I smile. "Yes. It's Sophie."

Chapter Seventeen

I smooth out my cherry-red dress as I walk down the stairs to join the gathering of my friends and family. There are waitresses walking around and serving hors d'oeuvres and glasses of wine on little platters.

"Helen, where have you been?" Liam calls out when he sees me. "James just arrived! Almost everyone's here."

Liam looks so excited as he holds a wine glass in one hand, and wraps the other arm around the shoulder of his judo teacher. James smiles and waves at me, and I smile back before glancing at Owen. He looks very anxious as he stands beside Carmen, with his arms crossed and his eyebrows knitted. I give him a small nod to indicate that I was successful, and some of the tension leaves his shoulders.

"I was just getting some last minute writing done," I say as I reach the bottom of the staircase. I couldn't very well tell Liam that I was making phone calls to California and trying to convince a complete stranger to come to our wedding.

"You need to give the writing a break!" Liam says with a laugh. He turns to James and the other guests with a shake of his head. "I swear, she intentionally does this to drive me crazy. When Helen actually sets aside time to sit down and write, she procrastinates and does anything *but* write. But try to get her to go outside or do anything at all, and it's a writing bonanza. Take her to the gym, and she's suddenly sitting on a weight lifting bench and writing on her phone."

"That sounds like my little girl," my father says fondly.

"I'm not really that bad," I say a little defensively. "But I don't see why I shouldn't take advantage of the fact that I can work from anywhere!"

"She was writing the whole time yesterday when we got our pedicures," Carmen adds with a laugh. "So much for spending quality time with my sister!"

"You were on your phone, too," I say glumly.

"I think it's great," Leslie adds. "I feel less guilty about making my patients wait when they actually have things to do in the waiting room, and don't just despise me for wasting their time. Really, they're just wasting their own time by not bringing something productive to do."

"Exactly!" I say with an enthusiastic nod. "Life is too short to waste precious energy not working hard, or playing hard—and when you're too exhausted from all of that, then you can rest."

"Wait until you get older," Leslie says with a smile. "You'll have to add 'relaxing hard' to your list of things to do."

Liam nods. "I've already had to do that. Sleeping pills."

"I am pretty sure that's just for doctors. Writing is already somewhat relaxing. Unless I'm on a deadline," I tell them with a smile.

"Don't go near her when she's on a deadline," Liam warns. "The whole world ceases to exist, and all that matters is her story. Sometimes I think that if I didn't feed her, she would chew off one of my limbs and go back to writing."

Everyone laughs at this, and I nudge Liam with my elbow, sending him a glare for making fun of me.

"That's why I always say that writers are totally insane," says a new voice from the doorway.

"David!" I say with excitement, moving to greet him. I am intending to give him a hug until I notice that there is a leash in his hand, and another old friend is trotting up the path to the house. Dropping to my knees, I extend my arms to the puppy. "Snowball!" I exclaim, completely forgetting that I am wearing an expensive cocktail dress that Carmen picked out for me.

The puppy jumps into my arms and begins licking my face, destroying the makeup that Carmen carefully applied earlier. Laughing, I hug her against me and stand up. "Is she my wedding present?" I ask David. "Do I get my dog back now?"

"Sure, but if you hear about some guy on the news who hung himself because he couldn't cope with losing his wife, his dog, and his new dog, then you'll know it's me."

Rolling my eyes, I turn back to look at the room full of our guests. "Everyone, I'd like you to meet David Duncan. He's a painter who obviously has issues, obviously needs therapy, and really should stop stealing people's dogs."

Snowball yips in agreement.

"At your service," David says with a mock bow.

"Good to see you again, man," Liam says, moving forward to shake David's hand. "You remember Owen? This is his girlfriend Carmen, who is also Helen's sister. This is their father, Richard Winters, and his girlfriend, Dr. Leslie Howard. This muscular fellow over here is James, a judo champion and amazing instructor who is responsible for turning me into a tough guy."

"A lot of the doctors in the room," David says as he takes a glass of wine from the tray of a waitress. "I suppose that means I can drink all I want, and someone will have the technical skill to save me from alcohol poisoning and death."

"I wouldn't count on it, young man," Leslie says with a smile. "This is the rehearsal dinner. We're all getting drunk tonight!"

"Come on," Owen says, moving closer to us.

"I'll show you to your room, David, and you can get settled in."

"Awesome, man. I'll just grab my suitcase from the car."

As Owen moves past me to help David, he fixes me with a worried look. "I hope you know what you're doing," he whispers, softly enough that no one else can hear.

But Snowball does, and she bares her teeth a little and growls at Owen, as if to tell him that he should be more positive and optimistic about this.

Chapter Eighteen

"Wow," James says, holding his stomach. "That was one of the best meals I've ever had. In my whole life."

"We got lucky with the caterers," Liam says modestly.

That's a lie. We painstakingly researched the best caterers and chose one with an incredible chef who uses fresh, superior quality ingredients.

"And this is only the rehearsal dinner!" Owen adds, leaning forward in excitement. "If the food is better tomorrow, I think I'll die of happiness."

"I hope you all saved room for dessert," I say as the waitresses enter the room with the final course. One of the girls moves to the table to begin pouring everyone's glasses full of port. I am really in love with the port selection we made—it is hands-down, one of my favorite wines, although I don't drink it often to save it for special occasions. This particular bottle is a 40-year-old port with notes of figs and honey, and we've paired it with a decadent chocolatey dessert.

Loretta Lost

I love desserts that do things. The chocolate is served in the shape of a large, closed rosebud, on a bed of chocolate leaves and decorations. The waitresses then pour warm liquid chocolate on the top of the dessert, to release the individual chocolate "petals" and allow the flower to unfold, as though it is blossoming. This reveals the actual dessert within the center: a lychee-flavored crème brûlée, with dulce de leche on the side.

Looking around the table, I feel my heart swelling in pride as everyone exclaims in amazement as their desserts unfold. All those hours spent researching cool desserts on YouTube while I should have been working suddenly feel worthwhile. I need to take a deep breath to keep from getting emotional; only a year ago, I never would have been able to experience my food with my eyes. I never would have been able to request having something like this created. The visual pleasure one can obtain from food is still surreal to me, and I sometimes find myself close to tears over something as simple as a wine bottle.

It's art. Food is art, just as much as my writing or David's painting. And the presentation of the food is nearly as important as the food itself.

When I take a sip of the 40-year-old port, tears do come to my eyes, but I struggle to keep them unshed. I am not even a wedding person! I don't know why I went so overboard in some ways. When I take a spoonful of the crème brûlée, I shut my eyes in pleasure momentarily, and then open them for several more bites.

Tomorrow's dessert, after the wedding, will be served in ice frozen in the shape of hollowed-out hearts. I know. I really need to step away from the YouTube.

"This is really incredible, Helen," Carmen breathes in awe as she stares at her dessert. "Growing up, I never thought you cared about getting married or having a wedding. And the guest list was so small that I thought you were going to be lazy and cheap, but you really did an amazing job."

"I didn't care. Until I found the right person to marry," I say softly.

Liam grasps my hand under the table, and we smile at each other, until I need to look away in fear of being way too cheesy. Speaking of cheese, the wine and cheese pairings I have set up for tomorrow are to die for. A strange thought crosses my mind:

I hope that Sophie likes it.

I wish that she didn't have to miss this dinner tonight, but I suppose it is more dramatic for her to show up on the day of the actual wedding. Besides, this will give Liam time to relax and mellow out in time for his major surprise. I glance at him warily, as he begins chatting with our guests, and I can't help wondering what his reaction will be.

Did I screw up? Did I overstep my bounds? Somehow, I don't care. I know, deep down, that this is the right thing to do. I only spoke to Sophie on the phone for a few minutes, so it was difficult to get a read on her, but she seemed intelligent, sweet, skeptical, and damaged. Her voice echoes in my mind, and I replay her conversation.

I... had given up on ever finding my family. Are you absolutely sure he wants to meet me?

He does. The problem is, he doesn't know you exist. He thinks you died when you were an infant, and he thinks it's his fault. It's been eating him up for years.

Was I convincing enough? Is she really going to show up? What if she turns back at the airport or changes her mind? I can only imagine how afraid she is.

"It's too bad neither of your parents could make it," my father is saying to Liam, who is looking down at his plate.

"It's probably for the best," Liam says. "My parents aren't great dinner guests. I'm just glad that Owen and James are here. Thanks for making it all the way out here, guys."

"Yes, it means so much to us," I say with a smile.

"Are you kidding?" Owen asks. "We're the lucky ones, to get pampered with all this great food and a free weekend stay in a cozy bed and breakfast!"

"This place is beautiful," Leslie says with a contented sigh as she sips on her port. "You've really outdone yourself, Helen. Getting married here was a brilliant idea."

"Speaking of which," Liam says as he dabs his lips with a napkin, "I would like to take my wife-to-be on an evening stroll among the grapevines. It's a beautiful night, and I think we should get some fresh air after all the hectic wedding prep we've done over the past few days."

"That sounds really nice," I say in surprise.

"Just bring her back before midnight," my father says playfully. "The bride is going to need her beauty rest!"

"I will," Liam says with a respectful nod of his head. When he stands up and bows slightly from the waist while offering me his hand, there is a moment when I am sure that he is a fairytale prince.

It's probably just the wine talking, but I have to blink the image away as I take his hand, and wonder how he can be so impossibly charming. Of course, I immediately ruin any possibility of being mistaken for a fairytale princess by grabbing the expensive port and tossing it down my throat.

"Let's go," I say happily, with the dizzying flavors and aromas still swirling on my palate.

I allow Liam to guide me out of the house from the back entrance, and we stroll toward the lake.

"I was just feeling a little crowded in there," he explains. "Plus all the talk about my family…"

"Of course. I understand. The fresh air is exactly what I need, too."

We keep walking and gazing at the scenery, when he clears his throat to apologize.

"I probably should have grabbed our coats. It's getting a little chilly out here."

"The wine is keeping me warm for now," I assure him.

He smiles and puts his arm around my waist. "We could always keep each other warm."

"Let me take you to a good spot by the lake," I tell him, grabbing his hand and guiding him. I wonder if it will still be there? It was my favorite spot as a child. I close my eyes briefly as I lead him, but it is too beautiful out to keep them closed for long. Even with my inferior vision, I can see the reflection of a waxing moon on the water.

"Here we are," I tell him, after a few minutes of walking. "Carmen and I used to read under this tree for hours."

"It's beautiful," Liam says, collapsing onto the grassy ground. "Would you believe all these stars? I can actually see the freaking Milky Way."

I rub my eyes, trying to see what he does, but my vision will never be that sharp. Sighing, I lie down beside him and rest my head on his shoulder. "Why don't we get away from the city more often? I like it so much better out here."

"If we were always out here, then we wouldn't appreciate it as much when we do manage to escape."

"That's a good point."

We lie together in silence for a moment, and my thoughts travel to his sister. I know I should just let it be a surprise, and see how he reacts tomorrow, but I can't resist saying something. I am just so afraid that he will be angry. If she shows up, I will

150

have to explain that I stole his sample for the DNA test.

"Liam," I whisper against his shoulder as we lie in the grass. "Is there anything that could make you change your mind about marrying me tomorrow?"

"Nothing at all. Not even if you were born a man. I would just thank the doctor who constructed your female parts, because he's obviously a genius."

"I'm serious, Liam. I've done something— something I'm not proud of. I don't know if you're going to be able to forgive me."

"Helen," he says with a smile. "You're taking advantage of the fact that I'm drunk right now and there's a good chance I won't remember any of this in the morning. That's not fair. You're supposed to be taking advantage of my body and making love to me under the stars."

Sliding my hand over his chest, I sigh. "Maybe. But something's going to happen tomorrow; something that could change everything.

"Our marriage? Yes, it will change everything."

"No," I tell him softly, "something *else.*"

"My love, this is not the time for fear and doubts. I am feeling really good, buzzed on fine champagne, and high on life. I assure you that there is nothing on the planet that could prevent me from marrying you."

"What about off the planet?" I ask with a

nervous smile.

"Let's see. There aren't any sexy girls at the International Space Station, but if we take into account all the potential alien species out there—I guess there could be a devastatingly beautiful green female with the power to tempt me away from you. As an ophthalmologist, I do find six eyes way hotter than two." Liam's hand has been moving up and down my side, but now it slides down to cup my bottom and gently squeeze. "You'll just have to give me a really good reason to stay here on Earth, won't you?"

"What would make you want to stay?" I ask as I wrap my leg around him and snuggle closer.

"Hmmm," he says thoughtfully. "It might begin to convince me if you'd take off this tantalizing red dress, and let me taste every inch of you." His hand moves to my back and grasps the top of my zipper and slowly slides it down to release the fabric from around my body.

The cool night breeze wafts over my exposed skin, and I shiver slightly. "Well, if that's what it will take... I'll do anything to keep you interested."

"You Earth girls are so eager to please," Liam says huskily as he fumbles to unclasp my bra. "Only two breasts instead of three or four? Not that interesting. Can you make it up to me by being a really bad girl?"

"I'll try my best," I say softly, slipping my dress off and moving to straddle him. I haven't had too much to drink, but it seems to have been just enough wine to make me tingly and warm on the inside, and to make this ridiculous little role play feel ridiculously sexy.

Liam moves his hands up to knead and massage my breasts until I moan. "You're so spoiled, with all your water, and oxygen, and... trees. I should teach you a lesson," he says, as a mischievous smile settles on his lips.

I smile too, and can't help but think to myself, *I'm marrying this goofball. How did I get so lucky?*

I feel like there is something serious nagging at the back of my mind that I wanted to discuss with him, but when he puts his hands on me like this, I have trouble thinking. "Liam," I say softly as I grab his wrists to halt him. "Are you sure that..."

"Shhh," he says, putting his hands around my waist and lifting me down onto the ground. "You need to stop stressing out, Helen. Everything's going to be fine."

"You promise? Promise you won't be mad at me, no matter what happens tomorrow?"

"I could never be angry at you," he tells me as he positions his body over mine and kisses me deeply on the lips. "Now will you give me a sneak peek of what it will be like to be married to an Earthling woman? I've always wanted to know if they're as insatiable as the rumors say."

Lifting my hands to his waist, I undo his belt buckle and the button of his pants, quickly fumbling to pull them down. "I don't know about other Earthling women, but you're going to have to work real hard to satisfy me, Dr. Larson."

Chapter Nineteen

I am standing by the road in my wedding dress, and tapping my foot anxiously.

She should be here by now. Is she going to show up? I don't know why, but I feel like it will totally crush my heart if she doesn't come. Poor Liam has such terrible luck with family, and I want so badly for this one girl to change all of that for him.

Maybe he'll see that family can be a good thing. That it could be okay for us to have children together, and potentially lead to a lifetime of joy instead of heartache.

The wedding was supposed to have started already. No one except for Owen knows why I delayed, and I'm worried that Liam is growing upset or suspicious. Does everyone think I'm bailing? I don't care.

I suppose I understand how nervous most brides feel on their wedding day, even though I am nervous for all the strangest reasons. I have no concerns about walking down the aisle to marry the love of my life, but I am worried that I may have sabotaged myself. My last minute invitation to Sophie has filled me with dread and excitement; how will they interact? Will they like each other? This will either be the best day of Liam's life, or one of the worst.

I don't know why it bothers me so much that Liam doesn't have any relatives at the wedding. It just doesn't feel like a legitimate wedding without family there to witness the proceedings. This is why I jumped through hoops to get Sophie's contact information, and beg her to get on a plane as soon as possible. I hopped on Expedia and got her a plane ticket, and sent a car to the airport. I did everything possible to make this happen in time for the wedding.

So she should be here. Any minute now.

I shut my eyes and silently pray to anyone who might be listening. I hear the sound of an engine before I see the vehicle approaching. Squinting to see it more clearly in the distance, I begin to hold my breath, and my heart starts beating faster.

When the town car pulls up in front of the winery, I don't care that I am wearing my wedding dress as I run up to the vehicle. The door opens slowly, hesitantly, as the girl steps out. She is wearing simple black pumps and a stylish black pantsuit. She has a small carry-on suitcase of luggage with her that she removes from the cab.

Her dark hair is curled and her face is intelligent. Even though her hair and eye color are not the same as his, there is something about the shape of her face and nose that reminds me of Liam.

"I'm Helen," I tell her softly.

"Sophie," she says apprehensively, staring into my eyes.

We size each other up for a moment. She is a little taller than I am, but not by much. Both of our facial expressions are calm and guarded, and I feel surprisingly good about her. Reaching out, I grasp both of her hands in mine, and give her a genuine smile. I can feel that her hands are shaking with nervousness, even though she is trying to conceal her emotion.

"Thank you *so much* for coming to my wedding," I tell her with all the strength I can manage. "Your brother is waiting for me at the altar."

"He doesn't know about me?" she says, and her voice wavers.

I shake my head to indicate the negative as I release her hands. "No. I didn't feel… I didn't want to tell him unless I knew for sure that you were going to be here. I didn't want to upset him today, or get his hopes up if you decided you didn't want to meet him."

"Okay," she says quietly, nodding and straightening her posture. "Let's do this."

She is strong. Her face is pale, and I can see that she is terrified, but she is also strong. I nod, and wave the taxi away before stepping toward the house. "You can leave your luggage here for now," I say, gesturing to the front of the house. "There's no one around for miles. The wedding is taking place in the backyard."

"It's a little strange," Sophie says. "To meet my brother for the first time on his wedding day. At his wedding. I feel like I'm intruding. Should I just hang back over here while you get married, and introduce myself after?"

"No way," I tell her. "He doesn't have any family here except for you. He needs you to be here, even though he doesn't know it yet.

Sophie pauses and tightens her grip on the handle of her luggage. "I have never known anything about my family," she tells me hesitantly. "Are my parents here, too?"

"No," I respond. "Your brother didn't want to invite them, because… well, they're not good people. They live in New York City, and we can arrange for you to meet them as soon as possible, if you want."

"I do want," she says, and I see her jaw set with a bit of hardness. I can't imagine what she's been through, and how she feels about all this. I suddenly feel very spoiled and grateful to have my family, and to have grown up with all the luxury that I've had.

I notice that Sophie's fingers holding the luggage handle are turning white.

"Come on," I encourage her gently.

"Whatever happens, there's an amazing lobster dinner after this, and an open bar where we can get wasted."

Sophie smiles. "Okay," she says, releasing the luggage. She begins following me along the path that runs beside the house, and to the backyard.

As we approach, I see that everyone is looking at me with puzzlement. Except for Owen. No doubt, he was keeping everyone calm while they worried about my whereabouts.

"I apologize for holding up the ceremony," I tell everyone as we approach, "but we were missing one guest."

"Helen, what's going on?" Liam says with a frown. "We were supposed to start fifteen minutes ago, but Owen said that you…"

"It's okay. I'm here now, and I'm ready to get married. I just wanted to seat our final guest."

Liam's eyes narrow as he turns to look at the girl who is standing beside me. Sophie holds her head up proudly and meets her brother's gaze, but I can see that her lip is slightly quivering.

"Who is this, Helen?" Liam asks me, leaving his spot at the altar and moving toward us slowly. "What's going on?"

I take a deep shuddering breath as I view Liam's face and his reaction. "Liam, this is…"

"No," he says softly, pausing in mid-step. His face displays some kind of recognition, and he shakes his head as he stares hard at Sophie, as though he is seeing a ghost. "This is—she is—who is this person, Helen?" His forehead is deeply creased, and his lips are pulled into a tight line.

"My name is Sophie," she says quietly, and her voice sounds less confident than it was before.

I see Liam's Adam's apple move with swallowing as he turns to look at Owen, before looking back to me, and then to Sophie. He moves a hand to his forehead where the tension must be giving him pain. "You look like—" he begins, then he pauses and shakes his head, trying to gather his composure.

"I'm so sorry," Liam says finally, taking a deep breath. "I must seem like a blithering idiot. You just remind me of someone. You look exactly like my mother did when I was younger."

"I do?" Sophie says, and her voice breaks. She places a hand against her chest. "Really? I do?"

"Liam," I say softly, pushing past the lump in my own throat. "This is Sophie Shields. She is your little sister."

The backyard grows very silent then, except for the flapping of wedding decorations in the wind. Liam's face grows very pale, and he takes a staggering step forward. Knowing him, and loving him, has caused me to be able to feel what he feels, and I think my own chest might burst. There are tears pricking the back of my eyes, and I don't know how he can even remain standing.

He is unable to speak. He stares at me for a moment in bafflement, before turning back to the girl standing beside me. The tension in the air feels heavy, like we are all suspended in invisible molasses. Liam finally begins walking toward us briskly, until he is standing directly before the girl and towering over her. I look over nervously, hoping that she won't be intimidated by his size, but she doesn't move an inch.

This girl is tough. She would have to be, in order to survive what she has, and get by in this world with zero family to speak of. I already admire her.

"Clear blue eyes," Liam whispers in a shaky voice. He lifts his hand a little, as though he intends to touch her cheek, but he does not touch her. His fingers are shaking. "Just like in my dream. The neurologist was wrong. He said it wasn't real. But you're real."

Sophie's face remains nearly expressionless as she tries to appear strong, but I see a tear shimmering in her eye. "You remember me?" she asks hoarsely.

"Barely. Just barely. I was there when you were born, and I held you—for a moment." Liam shakes his head and looks up at the sky. "Oh my god, what have I done?" His face is twisted up and contorted in pain as he looks back down at Sophie. "I'm so sorry. Oh, god! What have I done? I'm so sorry. I'm a fucking monster. I could have killed you. I could have killed you."

The tears spill out of Sophie's eyes, and she moves forward to wrap her arms around her brother. As soon as she does this, Liam begins sobbing and hugs her back, so tightly that I fear he might crush her. My own tears begin to fall as well as I watch them embrace. Owen moves to my side and squeezes my hand reassuringly, and I smile at him through my tears.

"It's okay," Sophie says softly, as she comforts Liam. "It's okay."

"I thought you were just a dream," Liam says into her shoulder as he clutches her tightly. "All these years. I thought—I thought…"

"It's okay," she says again, soothingly.

"I tried to make her go back for you. My mother said there was no baby. She said—she said you weren't real. Oh, god. This is all my fault. I'm a fucking monster."

"No," Sophie says, pulling away and looking at him with an expression that is somehow filled with power. "You were just a child. You were innocent in all this."

"I knew it was wrong. I could have done something if I'd tried harder. I left you. I just left you there. You could have died!"

"You're my brother," Sophie says softly, "and if it weren't for Helen, I would have lived my whole life without meeting you. All I feel—all I feel is happy. Happy to know something about where I come from, and who I am."

"Happy?" Liam says. "After what I've done?"

"Yes," she says with strength in her voice. "I forgive you."

She leans forward to hug Liam again to

emphasize her words. He hugs her back tightly, until he comes to his senses and looks at me. "Helen. You did this? How? How did you find her? Owen? You're in on this too."

We both nod.

"I'm sorry," I tell him softly. "I know you didn't want me to do the test. But remember that night you drank too much? The surprise bachelor party? I asked Owen to…"

"You stole my DNA?" he asks in shock.

"Yes, but…"

"Owen, you helped her do this? You—you drugged me," Liam says in sudden realization. "You drugged me so you could steal my saliva. What kind of a friend are you?"

"Dude, I'm sorry," Owen says, moving forward to put a hand on Liam's shoulder, but Liam grabs his wrist and twists it, roughly shoving his friend away. "Ouch!" Owen says in pain, rubbing his wrist.

Liam turns to look at me harshly, and there is a flash of something I don't recognize in his eyes.

In an instant, before I can realize what is happening, he is moving briskly toward the house.

"Liam!" I call after him in surprise. This is not how I imagined my wedding day going. Even with the curveball of Sophie thrown at us, I hoped that Liam would be happier than ever to meet his long lost sister, and that we would have an even more emotional wedding. But now, I am staring at my fiancé's back as he walks away from me. After a stunned second of simply staring, I remember that I have legs.

"Liam!" I call out again, picking up the gigantic skirt of my dress and running after him. I have a dreadful feeling in my gut that he is going to do something he'll regret.

When I get to the house, I enter the back door and through the rooms quickly. I see that there is a block of knives that has been knocked over in the kitchen. "Liam!" I yell out in panic, afraid of what he might do. When I hear the roaring of an engine, I know that the sound belongs to Liam's BMW. I run to the front of the house where the cars are all parked off to the side, just in time to see the dust that has been kicked up by the departing vehicle.

Oh, god. Driving while emotional is never a good idea. I should know. Running all the way out to the road, through the cloud of dust, I stare down the empty highway in the direction that he would have left. I see rubber markings on the pavement, but the car is already out of sight. At least it's out of *my* sight, which is not very strong.

Turning back to the house, I move weakly and slowly, in a daze. All the wedding guests are now filtering out of the house, to see what happened. My father and sister rush over to me to give me hugs and fuss over me, but I don't hear their words. I lean against my father, while squeezing Carmen's hand for support. I feel so numb and disbelieving. "Car keys," I mumble. "Who has car keys? Someone, give me your car keys!"

"You can't drive in a wedding dress!" Carmen tells me firmly. "It's pointless to go after him."

"Can someone else drive?" I ask weakly. "Please."

"Uh, we could," David says as he crouches down to look at his car, "but your dashing doctor thought of that, and he slashed our car tires. I could put on a spare, but it wouldn't get us all the way to New York. Even if I call AAA, we'd still need to get the right tires at an auto shop."

"Dammit!" I curse.

"I'm sorry," Sophie says with wide eyes. "Oh my god, if I had known I would ruin your wedding, I never would have come. This could have waited a day. Or a week, or a month. I've already waited my whole life."

"No!" I say, weakly moving over to her and giving her a hug. "It couldn't wait another fucking *second!* I wasn't about to marry him while keeping this secret—that would be unforgiveable. I would hate myself. His reaction would have been the same, either way. He's just being a fucking baby!"

"Helen," Leslie says in a calm voice, as she takes a sip from a wine glass that she must have grabbed on her way through the house. "You know Liam well. What do you think he's going to do?"

"I think he's going to confront his mother," I respond in a tired voice. "He's angry. His father will probably say something offensive and demeaning to Liam, like he always does, and maybe even take a swing at him, like he always does… and

165

Liam, in this mood? He'll probably kill the bastard."

Chapter Twenty

Everyone has been fussing over me as I sit in the sofa at the vineyard home. Carmen is sitting beside me, and trying to be comforting, while Sophie is sitting across from me and staring at me with apprehension.

"Do you really think he's going to kill my father?" Sophie asks.

"It's extremely possible," I respond. "Liam has a strong protective instinct. I don't think he was really angry at me. Or even his mother. He's angry at himself for hurting you."

"He was four years old," Sophie says in confusion. "He can't expect to be responsible for that."

"It doesn't matter. He feels responsible," Owen says, from where he's leaning against the wall a few feet away. "The thought of abandoning his little sister wrecked him so much that he hasn't been able to sleep without medication, and he's had to repeatedly tell himself that the dream wasn't real in order to get through the day. Now, he just discovered that it is real."

"But why would it start bothering him so much now?" Sophie asks.

Owen shakes his head. "It's always bothered him. He had that nightmare in college."

"We've been trying to get pregnant lately," I explain to Sophie with a sigh. "He couldn't think about babies without remembering that traumatic experience of killing a child—or what he thought was killing a child."

"Should we call the police?" Leslie asks. "Maybe send them to Liam's father's home, and prevent him from getting a murder charge."

"No," I say blankly. "We need to call someone we know and trust in New York to go there and stop Liam. Not the police."

"Liam won't kill anyone," James says, jumping in with quiet confidence. "His martial arts training was about mental strength in addition to physical strength. He has great self-control, and we should trust him to release his anger in the way he chooses."

"If my father is as awful as you all say, then I don't care if he dies," Sophie says. "I just wish that I could see him once, or speak to him once, before that happens."

"He's an evil man," James says. "He has put that boy through so much suffering. He abused him for years, and abused your mother in front of him—and then neglected them both for many more years."

Owen nods. "Maybe it was for the best that she abandoned you. She was probably trying to protect you. Whatever family you grew up with, it was probably way better than living with the Larsons."

"You don't know anything about how I grew up!" Sophie snaps.

Owen flinches, and everyone in the room turns to look at her in surprise.

She takes a deep breath and lowers her eyes. "I'm sorry. It's just—if she really wanted to get rid of me, why didn't she just give me up for adoption instead of dumping me in a ditch beside the interstate? Do you have any idea how it feels growing up, knowing you were so unwanted, so repulsive that your mother wanted to discard you the second she ripped you from her womb? When they found me, I had pieces of placenta on me, and my umbilical cord was flapping in the wind."

The room is hushed into silence, as everyone exchanges pitying and horrified looks.

"I—I have to go," Sophie says, standing up and moving to her suitcase. "I have work tomorrow. I'll call a cab and just head to the airport. Thank you for having me."

"Nonsense, young lady," my father says. "We have a lot of food here, and you are still going to be family soon, when your brother gets his head out of his ass. Please stay the night at least, and let's get to know you."

"Or at least fly to New York to see your

169

parents first," Owen suggests. "You know, while they're still alive. If you can get a flight soon, you could beat Liam there. It's a long drive."

"This has been hard on me," Sophie says, gripping her suitcase tightly again. "If they're still alive in a few days... maybe I'll make the trip to New York. This is just not how I expected things to be. For years I dreamed of meeting my family, and..."

She shrugs and begins moving to the door. "Thank you, Helen. I just... can't."

With that, she is gone.

"I am going to go to the airport with her," I decide. "I need to go after Liam. Carmen, run upstairs and get me a change of clothes, and my purse."

"Sure thing," my maid of honor says, moving off the sofa to do my bidding.

"I'm sorry that you all came out here for a wedding and no wedding is happening after all," I tell my guests.

"Hey, this was way more entertaining than a mushy-gushy wedding," David says with a grin. "Remember? I'm recently divorced. Not the biggest fan of love right now."

I smile weakly, and I am grateful to see Carmen coming down the stairs with a pair of jeans.

"Who says there isn't a wedding happening here?" my father says. "We've got the officiant, and the decorations, and the food." He reaches into his pocket and pulls out a velvet box, and pops it open.

"I've got this giant rock with Leslie's name on it. Anyone up for a recycled wedding? It's eco-friendly and good for the environment."

"Oh my god, Richard!" Leslie says with wide eyes. "This is how you propose to me? Do you really think I need the goddamned rock of Gibraltar on my hand? I'm not an eighteen-year-old schoolgirl."

"You could have fooled me," he says with a naughty wink. "So is that a yes?"

Carmen and I share shocked looks, and Owen begins chuckling softly.

Leslie sighs and nods. "Yes, you stupid old fool."

Everyone in the room begins clapping and laughing as Leslie and Dad hug and kiss. It's surprisingly endearing, and the timing is interesting. It's like having a birth and a death in the family on the same day. Bittersweet.

"Helen," my father says suddenly, turning to me. "Put on your jeans and head to the airport. You should go after Liam. He's going to need you."

I nod, standing up and moving forward to give my father a hug. "Congratulations," I say softly.

"Hurry up," Leslie says, touching my shoulder. "Try to catch up with Sophie. She seems like she could use a friend right now."

Chapter Twenty One

Dr. Liam Larson

As I pull up to the filthy apartment complex in Brownsville, the hatred and anger in my chest hasn't dissipated in the least. In fact, it managed to grow during the hours it took to drive over here, and I drove so fast that I managed to shave hours of time off the trip. I slowed down a little in populated areas, but on wide, open stretches of the road? I pushed my car to the limit, letting it show me what it's really capable of doing. It only fueled my anger.

Stopping my car on the road, I don't care that there are no available parking spots as I turn off the vehicle and exit onto the road. A car in the opposite lane has to brake to avoid me, and the driver honks. I don't care. I keep marching forward to my parents' apartment.

When I reach the door marked #3, I pound loudly with my fist. "Open up!" I shout. "Open the *fuck* up!" I wait for a full second before I step back and kick the door so hard that the wood splinters around the doorknob, and it swings open.

When I move inside the apartment, I am immediately assailed by a smell. "Ma…" I stop in the middle of calling out for my mother. How could I even call her that, after what she's done? "Janet?" I ask, moving forward. "Where the fuck are you!" Neither of my parents are in the living room. Moving to the bathroom, I rip open the door and I am startled to see my father lying on the ground in a pool of blood, urine, and his own feces. The smell is disgusting, and I lift my sleeve to cover my face.

"Pops?" I say, wondering if he is dead. I don't know how I feel about this. Do I actually care if he lives, or am I disappointed that I didn't get to kill him myself?

He groans slightly, alerting me to the fact that he is alive. He must have slipped and fallen while getting out of the tub, and he must have been lying here for days. I am not sure if it's the son in me, or the doctor, but I know he needs medical attention. But first, where is my mother?

Moving through the house, I finally find her huddled in a corner of the bedroom. She is rocking back and forth with wide eyes.

"Is he dead?" she asks, over and over again. "Is he dead? Is he dead? Is he dead?"

I stare at her in complete confusion, suddenly seeing my innocent old mother in a very different light. Did she do this to him? Did she push him against the sink or the tub?

Either way, all the anger leaves me. She's not right in the head. How could she be expected to be, after all the times my father has beat her into a concussion?

Turning around so that I don't have to look at her, I feel all the hatred leave my heart. These people are old and sick. There is nothing that I can say or do to achieve retribution for what they've done, to me... and my sister. I swallow. My sister. I have avoided thinking about her for most of the drive here, but now I realize that I have fucked up.

Maybe I wasn't responsible for abandoning Sophie when she was born.

But I am responsible for abandoning her today.

There is no point to seeking revenge now. We are no longer children. Our lives are completely in our own hands, and the only thing that can be done is to be good to whatever family we still have. And on the first day that I've been part of my little sister's life, I selfishly stormed out on her, putting my own anger above all else.

How am I any different from my mother? I'm worse. She doesn't remember my mother abandoning her, but I'm sure she has a clear image of my back walking away. I'm sure she has a clear picture of what a scared and weak person I really

174

am, and how I am incapable of loving her.

Or Helen. Who has done so much for me. I walked out on our *wedding*. She must hate me.

Or Owen. He's been the greatest friend.

Or anyone.

I realize that I have been clenching my fist so tightly that my palm is bleeding. Reaching for my phone, I dial 911 and shut my eyes tightly while waiting for someone to respond.

"911, what is your emergency?"

"I just visited my father's home, and it seems like he's had a bad fall."

"We'll send someone right away. What is your address?"

Chapter Twenty Two

Helen Winters

I lean against the elevator wall as I take it up to the floor of Liam's apartment. I am so tired. I had to take a connecting flight to get here, and both planes were delayed at their respective airports. I thought for sure I could get to the home of Liam's parents before he did, but by the time I got there, the apartment was empty. So I had no choice but to come back home, and hope for the best. Liam hasn't been responding to any of my calls or texts.

When I get out of the elevator and walk out into the hallway, I see a pile of boxes up ahead. My first thought is that someone must be moving, but then I realize that the boxes are outside Liam's apartment. My walk quickens until I get close enough to see that these are my belongings.

"Liam?" I ask, moving to the door and trying the doorknob. "What's going on? Are you really so angry at me for the DNA test?"

There is no response. I reach into my purse and pull out my key to open the door. I struggle with the lock for a moment until I realize that it's not going to work. Liam changed the locks.

"Liam!" I shout through the door, knocking on it loudly. "Seriously? You're kicking me out? You're not even going to talk to me?"

I put my back against the wall and slump down until I'm sitting on the floor. I pull out my phone and stare at it, thinking of who I should text to help me pack up my things. Everyone I know is back in Michigan. Except for maybe Krista, but I barely know her and she has exams. So, of course, I make the classic, pointless breakup mistake of texting the one person I normally go to for help:

> Liam, I accept that you're kicking me out, but can you please help me pack these boxes into my car?

Delivered

I am close to tears, and I know that the moment he opens that door, I'm going to throw myself on him and beg him to forgive me, and cling to him until he caves and un-kicks me out. But he doesn't respond, and I find myself staring at the door for several minutes.

> Please, Liam. Can you at least watch the boxes so no one takes anything while I carry them down one or two at a time?

Delivered

The text messages sound totally calm and reasonable. Surely he will cave and his gentlemanly heroic side will win out, and he will decide to help me. I just need him to open the door. That's all. I just need to touch him, and kiss him, and I know that everything will be okay.

I stare at the motionless doorknob for several more minutes. I even lie down on the floor to gaze under the door, but I don't see any shadows or feet moving around. He's not even near the door. I don't even know if he's at home. But he must be! He just... hates me.

Closing my eyes tightly to ward off tears, I feel my breathing become short and shallow. I am trying to stay calm, and gasping for breath as though I'm crying, even though I'm trying so hard to avoid being more of a mess than I already am.

I brought this on myself. I know that. I know

that I deserve this.

When my phone pings with a text message, my heart soars and I nearly drop it in my mad rush to read what it says.

It's not from Liam. My heart quickly sinks even lower than it was before.

But I read the text message anyway, because I really need a friend. Anyone who cares is a blessing right now. It's from David.

> Hey, Helen. I decided to fly to NYC too, just in case you needed me. Left Snowball with Owen and Carmen. Is there anything I can do? How's Liam?

I bite my lip before responding.

> He kicked me out.

Delivered

It takes David a second to respond, and I stare at the screen until he does.

179

That asshole. Just let me know where you are, and I'll be there as soon as I can.

I immediately feel a little better. The pile of boxes isn't that large, and I don't have that much stuff, but from where I'm sitting here on the ground, it looks like a mountain. My hands are shaking, and I know that even if manage to load up all the boxes into my car without dropping anything, I won't be able to drive in this condition. I will probably just sit in my car and cry.

At least if David comes here, I can have a shoulder to cry on, and an extra pair of helping hands until I feel better. I proceed to text him the address.

"It looks like these are the last two boxes," David says as he easily lifts them. "You doing okay?"

I nod slowly. This whole time, I have remained sitting on the floor beside Liam's door.

CLARITY

Every few minutes, I have knocked and begged and pleaded for him to let me in, like a total fool. My eyes are red and puffy from crying and my voice is scratchy from screaming.

"One last time," David says gently. "Try one last time, and if he doesn't respond… we need to get out of here and leave him to his misery."

I nod again. Placing my cheek against the door, I take a deep breath, knowing it is futile.

"Liam, don't you want to say goodbye at least?" I ask through the door. "Please. I know that I hurt you, but let's still be friends. All my stuff is in the car, except these last two boxes. I'm leaving, okay? I just want to see you before I go. I love you, and I just want to know that you're okay."

There is no response. I wait for a few seconds before turning to look at David. His face is filled with pity and understanding. He has been so patient and helpful through all of this.

"What do I do now?" I ask him.

He shrugs. "I don't know. What were you supposed to be doing?"

"I was supposed to be packing for my honeymoon," I tell him softly. "I guess that's not going to happen, now."

"Where were you guys going?" David asks. "Let me guess: Hawaii!"

I shake my head. "Paris."

"Ohhhh. Paris," David says with a nod. "The City of Love. A great destination."

We are silent for a moment longer, until

David clears his throat.

"Hey, you know what's embarrassing? I call myself an artist, but I've never been to the Louvre. That's like being a writer and never having read the classics, like Tolstoy or Harry Potter."

I stare at him blankly for a moment until an idea strikes me. "Wanna come with me? I have the plane ticket already and I don't think I could bring myself to travel alone right now."

"Why not?" David asks, as his face begins to brighten. "Maybe it could do us both some good. Your sister is dogsitting Snowball, so I'm a free man."

I finally manage to push my mouth into the shape of a smile. The idea does make me feel a little better. I have been looking forward to my honeymoon for months. Why shouldn't I go? I was honest with Liam about what I did. Maybe stealing the DNA sample was disrespectful of his wishes, but it wasn't entirely selfish. I may have done something terrible, but it caused good things to happen, too. Sophie is wonderful, and *I* am glad to have met her, even if Liam isn't.

Maybe getting the hell out of this country is exactly what I need right now.

Getting the hell out of this country with a single, sexy painter who has seen me naked could be even better. Putting my palm on the ground and pushing myself upright, I glare at my ex-fiancé's apartment.

"Last chance, Liam!" I shout through the

door. "You either let me in try to forgive me, or at least *talk* to me, or I'm leaving. For good. For real. I am not going to sit out here and cry for you like a pathetic little child."

When there is no response, it only confirms my decision.

"Fine," I tell David with a nod. "Let's go to Paris."

"One sec," David says, moving toward the door. "Hey, buddy, I just wanted to warn you that Helen's really vulnerable right now. If you don't want to risk losing her, you should really open the door. Because I'm going to be *so* fucking charming and caring and supportive, and completely take advantage of the fact that you're being a major douchebag to a girl who obviously loves you like crazy."

I hold my breath, wondering if these threats are going to work. If Liam won't open the door for me, will he do it out of jealousy? Men are often more easily motivated into taking action by empty jealousy than by love or devotion. They are more sensitive to the feeling of being threatened than willing to put in a tiny amount of effort to preserve a relationship.

But Liam doesn't respond.

"Are you sure he's in there?" David asks, and when I nod, he frowns. "Liam! Don't be a fool, man. I'm serious. A girl like this is one in a million, and you should be thanking Helen for what she did. Even if it sucked a little to find out about your sister like that, just be grateful you ever found her at all! What if you needed to do that DNA test for health reasons when you were like, eighty or ninety years old, and you learned you had a sister, but she had died years ago? Isn't it amazing that you found her while you are both still young, and can have some time together? Get to know each other? Not everyone has that chance! For thousands of years, if family members got separated, that was it! It was done. They'd usually never find each other again."

David is trying so hard, and it's endearing, I put my hand on his arm, and shake my head to indicate that this is pointless. Liam doesn't want to see me.

"Fine!" David shouts. "But you really hurt Helen. Don't think that I'm not going to swoop down on her like a vulture who smells wounded prey. I'm gonna make real sure she knows that even if *you* are too much of a dick to appreciate her, there are other men in this world who would be happy to worship the ground she walks on. It's her wedding night, isn't it? She's going to be so upset and distraught and broken up over what you did. A few drinks, and she is going to need some male comfort, don't you think? I think so. You know what I think? In order to try and forget you, and the heartless way you abandoned her, she's probably going to need a willing volunteer to fuck her brains out."

"David!" I whisper nudging him with my elbow. "That's going too far."

"Sorry. I had to try. If he's not going to come storming out of there now, to beat the stuffing out of me, then I don't think there's anything we can do or say. He needs time alone."

Taking a deep shuddering breath, I nod. "Thanks for trying. Let's just go."

"I wasn't totally exaggerating my intentions," David says with a wink as he carries the last two boxes down the hallway.

"I know," I tell him. "But I really just need a friend right now. I can't stand to be alone."

"That's the dictionary definition of vulnerable," he points out.

Chapter Twenty Three

I feel so numb.

Sitting on the plane beside David, he is chattering on about all the things he longs to do in Paris, and I can't hear a word he's saying. All I can see is the image of Liam's back walking away from me, and the pile of boxes outside his apartment. All I can see is the closed door in my face, and the sinking feeling of being completely shut out.

Everything inside me hurts, but I feel absolutely nothing at the same time.

"Looks like we're taking off," David says, as the plane finally begins moving.

I stare at the scenery below, thinking about how I ruined everything.

"Hey," David says, grabbing my hand and squeezing it gently. "Cheer up. Better to not get married at all than to be married for years like I was, and then have a divorce that rips you in half and totally rips your life apart. The earlier, the better!"

It doesn't feel better.

"Helen," David says gently. "Look at me. This is your honeymoon. You're having it with the wrong guy, but we're going to enjoy ourselves, okay? You need to make a real effort to *not* be miserable. Don't let Liam have all this power over you. Don't let him completely crush you. You're a strong, independent woman with your own life and you don't need him."

I nod slowly, and try to force myself to speak. "I'm sorry, David. I'm trying to be strong, but it's all so fresh. I'm getting there, okay? Maybe if I get some sleep on this flight, I'll have more energy when we arrive in Paris."

"Sleep all you want," he says with a smile. "Just don't get upset if I sketch you! I also have eBooks to read, and research to do on the best restaurants and attractions in France. I hope you don't mind a lot of stuff related to art. I'm not in Europe every day, and I feel like it's an opportunity to really get inspired by greatness and immersed in culture and romance."

"I'll go anywhere you choose," I tell him softly. "I would be happy if this trip can help your career in any way."

"It will. And it should help yours, too," he promises. "Writers and artists can't stay in one place. We absorb all the information and emotion from our surroundings until they are empty and dry.

We need new locations, new experiences, and new feelings to keep producing and creating."

I turn to look at David and slowly nod.

He smiles at me reassuringly. "Oftentimes, the worst things that have ever happened to you, the darkest and most painful moments of your life, can be the most important moments, the ones that shape you into who you were meant to be."

"Were you always this wise?" I ask him.

"Yes. I'm a world-class expert at surviving a broken heart. Didn't you know that? When it comes to breakups, I'm like Gandhi, or Buddha."

The days are passing in a blur. They're also moving far too slowly. I think we're supposed to be having fun, but I can't find enjoyment in anything. Every moment without Liam is agonizing. The delicious French food, the dazzling Museums, the gorgeous architecture. I just keep wishing I could share it all with him. But when I turn to my side to tell him about something, he isn't there.

I feel like I have spent ninety percent of my waking hours staring at my phone and hoping for a message for him, instead of experiencing the sights and sounds of Paris.

"This one is my favorite," David tells me as we stand in front of a painting at the Louvre. "God, can you imagine how long it took him to do this? The layers, the perfect blending of colors, the precise-yet-carefree brushstrokes! I've seen the painting a thousand times before, and spent weeks studying it in school, but there it is—the real life painting. The *actual* canvas that he *actually* touched. It's surreal."

Sometimes it's hard to focus on what David's saying, because of the chaos in my own mind, but I do understand that he's excited to be here as we walk through the massive museum. I feel like I am just going through the motions. I wish I could be a little more present for David's sake; I don't want to be the worst traveling companion in the history of the world. I can tell he is really trying to cheer me up, but I feel like I am just dead weight that he is dragging around.

He is an amazing guy; when we first got here, he decided to spend a few hours on the streets of Paris, painting the portraits of strangers for a few Euros. He said it was on his bucket list. Part of me wonders if I am actually having better experiences here with David than I would have with Liam, but it doesn't matter. I can't enjoy anything. I would rather be confined to a hotel room for a whole week, and never leave the bed with Liam, than experience all the art and culture of the world with someone who isn't Liam.

I guess this is what they call lovesick.

"This place is huge," David says as he looks down at the guidebook. "I can't leave without seeing a few Caravaggios, and the Venus de Milo. Is there anything you want to see, or need to see?"

"I don't know," I say as we continue to walk. "We can go wherever you want."

I allow him to guide me through the museum, and I look around aimlessly until a painting on the wall catches my attention. I tilt my head to the side slightly before moving over to it. "This is a blind woman?" I ask softly, examining the painting.

"Yes," David tells me. "It's famous for the way that the light catches the…"

I tune out his technical jargon as I stare at the painting. I chew on my lip thoughtfully, thinking about Liam. "This is all because of him," I say softly, fighting back tears. "I wouldn't be able to see any of these paintings if it weren't for him. He should be here. I should be able to tell him how much he's helped me, how much he's changed my life. I should be able to thank him. What have I done? He was so kind to me…"

I feel pathetic, because I can't hold back the onslaught of tears. David wraps his arms around me and I cry into his shirt. I think this is the first moment I'm really letting go of my emotions, since the breakup. It's like I've been carrying around this huge, black chunk of decaying matter in my chest, heavy and full of insects that were eating away at my insides. It was poisoning me, and I'm ready to let it go.

"He lied to you, too," David reminds me. "Even when I met you, and you didn't have your memories. He was lying to conceal important events that had happened to you, because he didn't think you could handle it. He began lying to you from the first moment you two met. I don't see why there's such a double standard, and if you make one mistake—that I don't think is a mistake, by the way—he gets to throw a hissy fit?"

"Do you really think," I ask as tears slide down my cheeks, "that what I did was right? Or acceptable? It was a huge invasion of privacy."

"No. You were nearly his wife. Isn't there biblical stuff that says husband and wives have one body?" David thinks for a moment. "'For this reason a man will leave his father and mother and be united to his wife, and the two will become one flesh.' There. If it's your flesh too, you can DNA test it. The bible says so."

"But we weren't technically married yet," I say with a sniffle. "And I'm pretty sure there's stuff about wives obeying their husbands that trumps sharing the same flesh."

"Semantics," David says with a wave of his hand. "Look, Helen. I don't know how to explain this to you. What you did—it was obvious you didn't intend to cause harm. In fact, you were seeking information that could potentially be used to prevent harm. Your intentions were good."

"The road to hell…"

"Shut up," David tells me with a smile. "I'm not going to let you make yourself into the bad guy here. Liam was a big baby, and that's it. Do you

191

know how fucking *hard* marriage is? If he can't get over this one very small thing, then there's no way he's marriage material. Marriage means forgiveness, and effort, and compromise, and sacrifice. It doesn't mean always getting your way, and running away if you don't."

"Thanks, David," I tell him softly, hugging him again. The tears finally subside. "Maybe you're right."

"You might have just escaped a miserable life with the wrong person," David tells me as he hugs me back, kissing the top of my head. "Divorce is torture, and I wouldn't wish it on anyone. Did I tell you that my ex-wife took my dog?"

"A few times," I say with a small smile.

Chapter Twenty Four

Three weeks later...

As we sit at a restaurant in Zürich, I realize that I am not checking my phone for messages from Liam quite as often as before. I am starting to really give up on him. I'm starting to move on.

"Do you want to try any of my smoked pork loin?" David asks me as he cuts it with a knife. "It's delicious."

"Sure, but just a small piece. I'm getting full on this fondue," I tell him as I dip a piece of bread into warmed up emmental cheese. The selection of various breads is amazing, and I can't help indulging, even though the DNA test warned me that I could develop Celiac.

David and I ended up extending the fake-honeymoon in France, because we both actually began enjoying ourselves. We decided to explore

193

more of Europe, and took a train to Luxembourg, then to Frankfurt, Germany, and finally, to Switzerland. The trains are so fast, and the distances feel so small. More importantly, the experiences are really enriching. I don't know why I didn't do this sooner.

When you're stuck in the U.S. for years, it can be hard to force yourself to leave the continent. But once you get out, and travel a little, it's hard to stop. It's easy to keep going and going to try and forget all the problems you left behind at home, and after a while, they do start to feel a little further away.

A little.

David's even managed to work on some paintings while we've been here. Sometimes I wake up in our hotel room to find sunlight streaming in through the windows and David painting me, which makes me feel embarrassed, but also makes me feel pretty and special at the same time.

We decided that since we are both artists, and capable of working from anywhere, there was no need to rush our return home. We've communicated with Owen and Carmen, and they don't mind taking care of Snowball for as long as we need.

I don't have any reason to go back to the United States.

Using my fork to stab the piece of the pork loin that David placed on my plate, I place the meat in my mouth and enjoy the flavor.

"Mmm," I tell him with a nod. "So good." The meat is sweet, and fatty, and delicate. But there's something about the smell that's a little funny. Ignoring this, I continue to eat my cheese fondue, until my stomach starts to churn. I put a hand on my chest, trying to will my stomach to be calm, but it won't listen to me.

"Are you okay?" David asks me with concern.

"Yes, I'm just feeling a little..." I can't finish my sentence, because I need to stand up and sprint to the bathroom. I am grateful that it is a clean bathroom when I quickly fall to my knees and vomit into the toilet. I upchuck the contents of my stomach for several seconds, before staring down into the bowl with horror. All the delicious bread I've just eaten is now floating on the water in the toilet bowl.

I reach up to wipe my sleeve across my forehead, because I've begun sweating.

The good news is that this probably isn't related to Celiac disease.

The bad news is that this probably isn't related to Celiac disease.

"Helen!" David says as he enters the girls' bathroom. "Are you okay? Was it the pork loin? I knew I should have ordered the sauerkraut..."

"David," I tell him weakly as I grab some tissue to wipe my lips. "Dammit. Dammit... *dammit!*"

"What, what's wrong?" he asks.

I look up at him, and shake my head, both amused and upset. This must be one of life's cruel tricks. To dump what you wanted right in your lap, but only when you no longer want it—and no longer have room for it in your life.

"I could be pregnant," I tell him softly.

"Oh my god." David crouches down to my side and wraps his arms around me in a comforting hug. "This explains why you've been crying so much. Hormones."

"Or maybe because I just broke up with my fiancé!" I remind him. "It's normal to cry a lot after a breakup. I thought you knew that, Mr. King of Breakups." Even as I say this, I am getting teary eyed again.

"Shhh," he says softly. "I'm so sorry. What are you going to do? Are you going to tell him?"

"I don't know," I whisper. "What if he doesn't respond, and doesn't care? I'd rather not tell him."

"I'm here for you," he tells me, gently cupping my cheek with his hand. "I hope you know that. I haven't been trying to get into your pants as much as I'd like to, because I don't want to be a jerk, but if you want me—I'm here for you. I could help you raise the baby, and I would love it like my own. I care about you Helen, and I love being around you. You make me feel whole, and alive, and like nothing bad has ever happened to me."

"I like being around you, too," I tell him, as tears slide down my cheeks.

"You're amazing, Helen. I see you kneeling on the bathroom floor with vomit on your face, and I just want to kiss you—but I won't, because we've both been through too much heartbreak, and I don't want to act without thinking first. If you want me, then I will be yours, and I'll never let you go. Just say the word, and we can be together," he promises me.

"Do you really mean all that?" I ask him in amazement.

"Yes. We could travel all over the world together. You know that my job gives me more freedom than a doctor could ever have. When we're at home, Snowball could live with both of us. We could be happy."

It's hard to focus on what he's saying, because I am so blindsided by the fact that there could be a little person developing inside of me. Everything else seems a lot less important, now. I need to do whatever's best for the baby. Would David be a good father? I don't know. He seems really devoted, and he is very intelligent. He's really been there for me these past few weeks.

And Liam hasn't said a word to me.

"Let me think about it," I tell him, tearfully.

Chapter Twenty Five

Dr. Liam Larson

"Open up!" my best friend shouts from outside my door. "Dammit, Liam! Open up!"

I think he's been there for three hours. This is the third day in a row that he's done this, and the neighbors are starting to complain. I don't know why he just doesn't go away. Why would he care about a piece of shit like me? I've been ignoring his calls and texts for weeks.

"Liam, I swear to god!" Owen yells. "If you don't open this door, I'm not your friend anymore."

That's Owen. He makes the threats of a kindergartener. Right now, it doesn't even make me smile.

I haven't shaved in weeks. I haven't showered. I have been lying in the same spot on the couch, and barely eating. I have been wearing the same dirty t-shirt and stained pair of sweatpants for weeks, and I smell worse than my father. I even watched the Kardashians a few times. I fucking hate myself.

"Liam, do you know that Helen went on *your* honeymoon with David? Do you know that they've been in Europe together for *weeks and weeks*? This doesn't bother you, man? If we don't head over there *right now,* he's going to steal her away from you. You'll regret it for the rest of your life!"

The thought makes me a little sick to my stomach, but I need to let it go. Maybe Helen will be happier with David. He's a good guy, and he isn't a monster like me. He never tried to kill a newborn infant.

I had some vacation days booked at work for our honeymoon, but after I ran out of days, I never went back to work. I have probably lost my job by now. I will probably lose this apartment once the money from work stops being deposited in my bank account. What does it even matter? I've already lost Helen.

The sound of a power drill startles me, and I lift my head from the couch abruptly, realizing that Owen is breaking into my apartment.

When he opens the door, he glares at me angrily. "Liam Larson! As your best friend and buddy forever, I cannot let you throw your life away! I *will not* stand by as you ruin everything. We are going to Europe *right now*."

"Owen," I say softly, when I see the concern

on his face. "It's pointless. I fucked it all up. I hurt Helen, and Sophie…"

"They all understand!" he basically shouts in my face. "It was an emotional day, of course you overreacted. Jesus, man! Stop being such a dramatic little girl. Stop moping around in your underwear and your *I'm-so-cool-I-don't-care-about-anything* beard. Let's go get Helen back! Sophie, too!"

Staring at him hopefully and fearfully, I shake my head. "Owen…"

"You know what? I've had enough of you feeling sorry for yourself."

Walking over to me, Owen swings his arm back and punches me in the face. Surprisingly hard.

My head swings to the side, and I open and close my jaw slowly, grasping the spot where his fist connected. "What the fuck, man?"

"You needed that, bro. Someone had to knock some sense into you. You can thank me later. We good? You gonna stop being a jackass and get on a plane now? Because I can hit you *all day long.*"

I blink as I stare up at Owen. He looks dead serious, and a little scary for the first time that I can remember. "She doesn't want me anymore. She hates me. After what I've done…"

"She's pregnant!" Owen shouts at the top of his lungs. "She's *fucking pregnant,* Liam!"

I blink at this news. I blink again. "It's… my baby?"

"Sweet holy Jesus, what do you think? Do you really think she had sex with anyone else when she's completely in love with you? Don't make me hit you again! No. They haven't slept together, Liam. I *wouldn't blame her* if she had, after what a jackass you were, kicking her out and putting all her stuff outside. I would have slept with David that same day if I were her, just to get back at you. I would have banged him *so hard*."

"This isn't helping," I tell Owen gruffly.

"My point is that you are lucky she's waited for you this long. But don't expect her to wait any longer, Liam. If you don't step up to be her husband and the father of her child—which, incidentally, you are—there's another man who will. And I think David's awesome, and if you want to leave it up to him to satisfy your woman, make her happy, and to provide for your child, that's up to you."

Owen steps away then, heading for the door. When he is nearly at the exit, he turns back, and gives me a disappointed and hurt look.

"But I can't be your friend anymore if you do that, Liam. There are only a few things I find unforgivable, and abandoning the mother of your child, and your unborn baby—I don't think I could ever look at you the same way again."

He is serious. For the first time in our entire friendship, he is serious. I can tell from the sadness on his face.

"Owen," I say hoarsely as tears flood my eyes. "I love Helen. I want the baby."

"I know. So, take a fucking shower, shave your fucking face—use a chainsaw if you must—

201

and get dressed! We're going across the pond to hunt down your woman."

"Okay," I tell him. "Fine. Okay."

Chapter Twenty Six

What am I even doing here? I am pacing back and forth across the hardwood floor of a romantic chalet in the Swiss Alps. I let Owen convince me to get on a plane to Switzerland, because apparently that's where Helen is now. He also rented a car and drove up to the mountains, past gorgeous landscapes that look like they belong on postcards. Apparently, Owen coordinated with David to bring Helen here, on the pretense that David wanted to go skiing and paint the mountains.

Why is David even helping me? Why would he even bring Helen here?

If he wants to steal her away from me, like he said before, then he should. I don't understand why he would participate in a plan to reunite us.

Owen said that if I could convince Helen to marry me again, that he would be the best best man on the planet, and plan an epic wedding right here in the Swiss Alps. I don't doubt his ability, but I do doubt my own.

"Hello, son," says the familiar voice of an

older man. I turn around to see Helen's father entering the chalet with his new wife, Dr. Leslie Howard, beside him. Owen filled me in on the plane about the way that they recycled our wedding, and I felt like shit for missing out on that, and making Helen miss out on her father's second wedding. Hearing the man call me 'son' also makes me feel like shit for not visiting my own father in the hospital.

"Mr. Winters," I say, nodding in greeting, and extending my hand.

The old man laughs and reaches out to give me a hug instead. "Call me Richard, boy. We're practically family, aren't we?"

I nod slowly, lowering my eyes. How can he still think that after I abandoned his daughter at the altar? How does he not want to cut off my head and toss it down one of these mountains, to be eaten by the goats?

"Hey, kid," Leslie says with a smile, as she moves closer. "Did you hear the big news? I'm just plain old Leslie Winters now."

My eyes narrow in confusion. "Don't you mean Dr. Leslie Winters?"

"Nope. I decided to retire and sell my practice. I bought up that gorgeous little vineyard in Michigan, and Richard and I are going to move out there and enjoy ourselves, making wine and getting messy. With the grapes, I mean."

"That sounds wonderful, Leslie," I tell her honestly. "I'm so happy for you two."

CLARITY

"Thank you, son," Richard says with a bright smile. "You and Helen are welcome to come spend holidays with us as much as you like. It's a great place for children to run around and play."

It hurts my heart a little to hear him speak about this future like it's set in stone. Doesn't he know that I destroyed everything? Doesn't he know that another man is probably going to raise my child, and I'm basically just a sperm donor? Doesn't he know that I've abandoned my own child, just like I abandoned Sophie all those years ago—just like I feared I would?

"Hey," says a female voice from behind me, and I see that the girl I was just thinking about has entered the room. Sophie walks toward me, wearing a fuzzy black coat over slim-fitting black pants that are tucked into black boots. "Are you ready to stop being a little princess now?" she asks me with arms crossed over her chest. "Because I'd really like to have a big brother."

"Sophie," I tell her softly, moving close to her. "You came all the way to Switzerland for me?"

"Not just for you," she says stubbornly. "Owen told me that Helen's pregnant, and if so, that means I'm going to have a niece or a nephew. I'd like to be part of their life, and actually have at least one person in this world I can call family."

"I want to be your big brother," I tell her brokenly. "I have from the moment I first held you in my arms. I wanted to play games with you, like checkers, and tag. I wanted to read stories to you at bedtime. I wanted to have a little sister more than anything, and when I was younger, I often dreamed that you were there. That we could build Legos together, or make a fort out of sheets. It just destroyed me to learn that you weren't just a figment of my dreams and imagination." Tears come to my eyes, and I shake my head. "Sophie, it hurts. All those years we could have spent together? Growing up together, and seeing all the big moments of your life happen. Beating up your boyfriends if they were jerks. I missed out on all of that."

"I still do have some boyfriends you could beat up," Sophie tells me, and there are tears in her eyes too. "It's never too late, Liam. I know that finding out that day was insane, and I understand that you needed to run. I've been running my whole life, from foster home to foster home, and from one state to the next. But at some point, you've got to just grow up and face the things you're afraid of. You're not a bad person. You can still be a good brother. And a good dad."

Moving over to her, I gather her up in my arms and give her the biggest hug I can manage. "Thank you," I tell her, kissing the top of her head. "Thank you for forgiving me. I don't know how I lived all these years without having you in my life. I'm going to make an effort to get to know you, and be there for you. And when we get back to the U.S., I'd like to meet those boyfriends of yours and have a few words with them."

CLARITY

Sophie laughs softly, and it's the most beautiful sound in the world. I have never heard her laugh before. Suddenly, I feel filled with hope and strength. I ruined this girl's whole damn life. I did that, with my own two hands. I could have killed her. I just dropped her there, and left her to die.

And somehow, she's standing here, and willing to love me?

I'll never understand the vastness of a woman's heart, and its infinite capacity to love and forgive. Neither the cavernous oceans nor the endless expanses of outer space could ever be as large.

When Owen returns to the room, he has Carmen with him, and she smiles at me.

"Hey, Liam," Carmen says happily. "Good job on getting my sister knocked up!"

"Don't congratulate me until I know for sure that she can forgive me," I tell Carmen softly.

"Just beg," Carmen advises, "and beg some more. And then beg again. Works every time."

Owen nods emphatically to second this advice.

Knowing that I have all this support from Helen's family, and our friends... and my own family, fills me with joy. I suddenly understand why Helen wanted so much for me to have a family member at our wedding. Family is the most important part of life.

The door to the chalet opens, and I turn anxiously, expecting to see Helen, but it is James and a girl I don't recognize. "James!" I say in surprise. "You made it all the way out here? Is this your girlfriend?"

"I'm Krista," she explains. "Helen's friend, from the hospital where you work. She invited me to the first wedding, in Michigan, but I had exams. So I figured I'd come to this one!"

"How did you guys all afford the trip?" I ask in amazement.

Helen's father laughs deeply. "You know that I've got deep pockets, son. I'm willing to do anything to make my little girl happy. And I know what would make her happiest is being with you."

"I hope you're right," I tell him softly. "Thank you all for coming. I hope that you won't be disappointed."

"They won't be disappointed!" Owen assures me. "If Helen rejects you, David will probably propose to her, and I can be his best man instead. Either way, we're having a romantic wedding in the Alps."

I stare at Owen in shock. "You would really be such a traitor?"

Owen shrugs. "I'm on Helen's team, bro. You ignored me for weeks until I had to break down your door. I'm not exactly your biggest fan right now."

My best friend's words remind me of what is at stake. If I can't convince Helen to marry me now, then I am going to lose her. If she's pregnant, her primary concern is going to be doing what's best for the baby. If she thinks there is any chance that I might abandon her again, I can completely understand her wanting to be with someone else.

But how can I say anything to convince her? Trust is built over time, through actions. Nothing I could say will be enough. How do I prove it to her? I think upon this for several minutes as everyone in the chalet chats about the beautiful scenery and catches up on each other's lives.

Finally, I hear voices approaching the chalet. I move to the window and see Helen and David walking up the path.

She's holding his hand.

She's fucking holding his hand!

My heart rate instantly doubles, as I imagine all the ways Helen could reject me. Does she despise me? Or has she fallen in love with someone else. I move away from the window and inhale sharply, feeling my blood pump through my body as though I have just finished running three miles. I briefly close my eyes, unable to face this moment.

When the door opens and Helen enters the room, the chatter abruptly stops. I look up in anticipation, eager to see her face. She is beautiful. It's been so long since I have seen her face. I hear her gasp a little and step back. Her eyes are filled with hurt and pain, and I know it's my fault. Stepping forward hesitantly, I try to think of the words to say. Apologizing feels so weak and small compared to what I've done.

Right now, we were supposed to be happy.

Loretta Lost

We were supposed to be together. Instead, I forced her to go on *our* honeymoon with someone else.

"Liam," she whispers, as tears fill her eyes.

Her hand is shaking, and she places it on her stomach.

All my reservations leave me in that instant, and I cross the room and wrap my arms around her waist. I lean down and place my lips against hers, pouring all my apologies and emotions into my kiss, kissing her desperately and passionately, and begging her to forgive me. Tears slide down my cheeks and onto hers, where our tears mingle. I kiss her so hard, and hug her so tightly that I lift her clean off the floor.

It takes a moment before I remember that we aren't alone in the room. When I break the kiss, her arms are around my neck, and she places her cheek against my chest, sobbing. I hold her so tightly. I hold her close, and pray that I never lose her again. I turn to look at David, and he is smiling at me. It's a sad smile, because he knows that he has lost Helen, but he also knows that he never had her.

But he nearly did.

David was never a factor in all of this. He isn't the reason that Helen and I aren't already married. He was just the only person she could run to for comfort when I shut her out. And if I hadn't come here, to Switzerland, today, I would have lost her forever. At some point, she would have realized that she needed to let go of me, and David was an excellent choice.

CLARITY

I just barely got here in time.

I smile back at him, to thank him for taking care of her.

"Helen," I begin softly, and my voice is gruff and hoarse. It sounds like I haven't used it in weeks. Probably because I barely have. "I love you. I'm sorry. I'm so sorry."

"I know," she tells me, with tear-filled eyes. "I know."

"You were right about the test," I tell her with a sad smile. "Now, I think I finally understand how you felt about your eye surgery. You always say that you're so thankful, but really, I was just doing my job. It was nothing at all. Anyone could have done that surgery on your eyes, but there aren't many people in the world who could care about me enough to discover that I had a sister. You have given me something priceless. You have returned Sophie to me, when she could have remained lost her forever."

I turn to look at my sister, who smiles and nods. My chest is full of love, and I can't help wondering what she's like. What has she been through since that day that we were separated? What does she do for a living? Why does she wear so much black? She seems smart, strong, and kind, but she also seems... lonely. Lonely and lost. I hope I'll get to know her soon.

Turning back to Helen, I take both of her hands in mine, before falling to one knee.

"Helen, you have given me a family. You *are*

my family. I've felt like a dead man, these past few weeks, being so far away from you. Will you please consider marrying me again? If I swear on everything that is holy that I won't fuck it up this time?"

"I—I don't know," she says suddenly, with confusion all over her face. "Liam, I'm pregnant."

"Owen told me. It's wonderful news."

"Gee, I wonder who told Owen?" she says, turning to glare at David, who whistles innocently.

"Are you sure you're pregnant, honey?" Leslie asks. "I'm so happy for you, dear!"

"Yes, Leslie—or should I say 'Mom'?" Helen asks with a smile. "I confirmed it with a pregnancy test called 'Maybe Baby' that I got from a vending machine."

"You got a pregnancy test from a vending machine?" Carmen remarks in surprise.

"I did. You can get the coolest things from vending machines in Switzerland!" She turns to look back down at me, and her smile disappears. "Liam, I'm just scared that you won't be there. Things get hard when you have kids. There's so much to do, and no time to make mistakes. I just don't want to be disappointed again by you walking away. I don't want my baby to be disappointed."

"God, Helen. I don't know if there's anything I can do to prove how much I want to be there for you and this baby. I couldn't live with myself if I wasn't there for all of it—to give you massages if you're in pain, doctor's appointments, the birth—

and even to change dirty diapers." I squeeze her hands harder. "If you marry me, I will do unlimited diaper changes from now until the end of time. That is how much I love you. I will never complain about the smelliness, because I will just be so freaking thankful that you are letting me be near our baby and our baby's wonderful poop."

"Really?" she says tearfully and happily. "Do you really mean it?"

"Yes. I will be there for you 110%, through thick and thin. I can't live without you, Helen Winters. If you aren't with me, I just fall to pieces. Please forgive me and come home."

"Liam," she finally says, nodding through her tears. "I will. Of course, I will. Do you know how scared I was? I thought I was never going to see you again." She stoops down to throw her arms around my neck, squeezing me tightly. "You're everything to me, Dr. Liam Larson. I need you in my life. You better be in this, 110%, because I'll kill you if you leave me again. Please, let's get married as quickly as possible, before you change your mind and have another temper tantrum. Also, I want that thing about the diapers in writing."

All of our friends and family in the room laugh at this, and I feel embarrassed, but I am too overjoyed to care. I would have stayed down on my knees and humiliated myself a thousand times for this woman before me, because she is worth every drop of pain.

Helen Winters is my soulmate.

Loretta Lost

I nearly lost her due to my own stupidity, but I will never take her for granted again. Thank god that I have a good friend like Owen, to save me from myself. He's the real hero of this story. Several years from now, when I tell my kids about how I ruined everything and nearly didn't marry their mother, they will laugh about that time when Uncle Owen punched Daddy in the face, and saved the day.

CLARITY

The End

Thank you for reading Clarity! Loretta enjoyed writing these books so much that she wanted to continue the story of Helen and Liam. A new series is now available, following Carmen's decaying state of mind in the aftermath of losing her husband.

end of.
eterNity

8

loretta lost

End of Eternity

Carmen Winters thought her life was getting better.
Until she came home to find her new husband
hanging from the chandelier.

Six months pregnant and devastated, Carmen is
forced to pick up the pieces of her shattered life. It
is only when she meets a sweet and sensitive
stranger named Owen that she finds herself able to
smile again. Is it really true that the best beginnings
can come from the worst endings? Or does Carmen
have deeper to fall before she can learn who she
really is?

Available from all retailers!

Subscribe to Loretta's mailing list to be informed of new releases.

www.LorettaLost.com

Connect with the author:

Facebook: facebook.com/LorettaLost
Twitter: @LorettaLost
Website: www.LorettaLost.com
Email: Loretta.lost@hotmail.com

Made in the USA
San Bernardino, CA
28 December 2016